Bruna and Her Sisters
in the
Sleeping City

Bruna and Her Sisters
in the
Sleeping City

ALICIA YÁNEZ COSSÍO

Translated from the Spanish by Kenneth J. A. Wishnia

NORTHWESTERN UNIVERSITY PRESS
EVANSTON, ILLINOIS

Northwestern University Press
www.nupress.northwestern.edu

Printed in the United States of America

ISBN 978-0-8101-4503-0

The Library of Congress has cataloged the original, hardcover edition as follows:
Yánez Cossío, Alicia, 1929–
   [Bruna, soroche y los tíos. English]
   Bruna and her sisters in the sleeping city / Alicia Yánez Cossío;
translated from the Spanish by Kenneth J. A. Wishnia.
   p. cm.
   ISBN 0-8101-1408-9 (cloth: alk. paper)
   I. Wishnia, K. J. A. II. Title.
PQ8220.35.A5B713 1999
863—dc21

                                                                99-39373
                                                                CIP

Contents

Prologue

Bruna decided to keep quiet, as always, and not to insist further. She had come from a city, had walked its streets, seen its golden churches with its belfries that got lost in the clouds, crossed its squares, in one of which they had raised a statue of her great-great-grandfather, who, even though he was a bishop, had 245 children. She had lived in the old family house, where she had learned to see life from a different angle. She knew the history of its inhabitants and the history of those who founded and built the city, but when she mentioned it, people asked:

"What city?"

"Where is it?"

And since it was difficult, humanly impossible, to explain the unexplainable, she chose silence.

People couldn't understand what had happened, and it was painful to explain certain details, so Bruna decided not to say a word.

"Where are you from?"

"Nowhere special."

"But where?"

"That way. . . . From the south."

With time, the silence gave her a certain superiority over people, as if she had lived her whole life high up in a tower and all humanity were there at her feet, listening to her say:

"I know a secret that no one else knows."

After she abandoned the city, everything was resolved with terrifying ease. She was twenty years old now, and she didn't have a past.

"How old are you?"

"Twenty. And you?"

"About the same."

"Then let's go."

"Where?"

"To the north."

She was completely free, on the broad face of the earth, so she decided to burn the ships of her shyness and hitchhike, with all of its problems and consequences.

Bruna felt happy; she had eyes that could look toward the future and the gift of being able to laugh at herself and at things.

"Are you happy?"

"Yes . . . I think so. . . ."

"Then let's go."

"Where?"

"To the east."

She liked traveling all around the world and making forays into her body mounted on a white blood cell, stopping in the fleshy middle of her heart, in the membranes of her brain, in the cobwebs of her insomnia.

She was happy when she was far from the city and its customs, inhabitants, and prejudices that kept her independence locked up.

She loved her new life, even though it was poorer than the one she left. She loved discovering new places, even though it was sometimes difficult. The difficulties of traveling were almost always economic, caused by fear of overspending in luxury hotels, where she felt so at home, as if she had been born for the mission of enjoying life; where nobody knew who she was, where she came from, and where she was going; if she were a fairy, a princess, or an imp, Ecuadorian, Russian, or Italian.

She discovered that fixed hours and schedules had no importance and learned the comfort of sitting on the hands of a clock as if they were an easy chair, without mealtimes, bedtimes, or wake-up times.

"What time is it?"

"I don't know . . . maybe five o'clock."

"Yes, five in the morning, or the afternoon, or Thursday, or Saturday, or Sunday."

The notion of time, of the accidental and irregular forms of the verb "to live," could all disappear, to be conjugated only in the present. The fullest and most wonderful freedom was to look out at the countryside through a picture window that seemed to have been placed there just to be looked out of at that moment. The people coming and going in the streets with the eagerness of ants, the cars going by like toys that had been wound up for the pleasure of watching them go, were all there so that a person with Bruna's possibilities could look at them and enjoy their true, splendid presence.

"Where are all the people going?"

"They're not going, they're coming. . . ."

"Where are all the people coming from?"

"They're not coming, they're going. . . ."

She learned the pleasure of giving herself to humanity, of talking to people who were traveling as she was. To talk of big things or little ones: politics, clothing, illnesses, art, hats, books. To feel the wonders of communicating, of racing through the interweavings of souls and reaching the spiritual realms, which were more interesting than the astral realms because they were generous, loving, superior—or wretched, confusing, or treacherous, depending on whether they were seen from her point of view or from others'.

"The first man has landed on the moon?"

"Yes, he's landed. . . . But 'he' has gone, and he hasn't come back yet."

Talking to people was an unexplored pleasure. Bruna enjoyed analyzing people's eyes, which spoke before their words. Hands that contradicted what the lips spoke. The unexpected blushing born in the pores of the skin, which rose through the temples and concentrated around the cheekbones, and whose true meaning was completed by gestures that took the place of ellipsis points.

"Pass the . . ."

"I know what . . ."

"You've got a . . ."

"That's how it . . ."

She enjoyed hearing sounds that never got formed by the larynx because the inner doors suddenly shut, although that didn't prevent her from penetrating another's psyche by a variety of other means, like the roots of the hair:

"No, she's not blond, she dyes it."

Through the fingernails:

"She works a lot."

Through a plunging neckline:

"No, she's not married, but . . ."

Or through the fabric of the stockings:

"She's trying to hide it, but she's bankrupt."

She learned of all the glory and misery of a world that was different in every place and at every hour, and she met human beings with full and open minds thanks to their will, words, bodies, and actions.

"Do you know me?"

"Yes."

"But, deeply, like . . . in the Bible . . ."

She liked the grand hotels where everything had its price: the air that penetrated the lungs regulated by the avid flaring of nostrils and that wasn't very fresh. The rugs that sank under the weight of bodies filled with memories and thoughts. The windowpanes; the smell, the color, the light of twilight seen through the windows; the people, all giving value to a place that was still cheap enough for them to be able to stay there.

When the money ran out she should have gone looking for cheaper places to stay, but Bruna couldn't free herself from her terror of miserable, flea-ridden hotels where suddenly, at midnight—

which is the precise hour for unwelcome thoughts—she was seized by the certainty that the sheets hadn't been changed because it was cheaper not to, which was the same as sleeping with a stranger, without being able to guess their precise sex, their nationality, their beliefs and ideology, or their native language.

"Who's slept here?"

"A man, a woman . . ."

"Maybe a Chinese; there're incense wrappers all over the place."

And she felt with the certainty of the things that one feels at that time of night that a germ, a microbe, a spermatozoa, had reached gigantic proportions, grabbed hold of her body, and devoured her, subdued her, made her disappear from the bed, from the room, from the earth, from memory.

Then Bruna got up, a bitter taste in her mouth, feeling a piece of her own liver between her teeth, her heart as agitated as if she were holding it in her hands. She bathed, if there was water, and let it flow over her skin in vertical streams that washed away bad thoughts and sadness. She sat in an armchair, if the room had one, and spent the nights reading a book, if one was handy; if not, she remained submerged in thoughts that she wanted to have in her head, casting out those that kept her stuck in the spaces between the untouchable, and yet being unable to because her mind was a vehicle always charting a course for the bewildering and unknown zone at the edge of the distant city.

"What are you reading?"

"A book."

"Which one?"

"*The Human Comedy.*"

"By Balzac?"

"No, Saroyan."

She waited for daybreak, and the hours lengthened as if they trailed never-ending cold and fog in their wakes that would keep the sun from rising and people from doing their everyday, mechanical things. It was a long wait.

"I didn't sleep last night. . . ."

"Me neither. . . ."

"What did you do."

"Nothing . . . and you?"

"Nothing either. . . ."

The world had shrunk to the size of the hotel room, even though there were other beings with the same anxieties and the same cravings who had to keep quiet, behind closed doors. The streets were dead; these were the hours that from time immemorial had been set aside for resting, and there was nothing else to do but wait.

Bruna waited, dreaming of the possibility that they would create, cozy and friendly places where people who suffered from the sickness of insomnia could meet.

"I can't sleep."

"Me neither."

"I suffer from insomnia."

"Me too."

"What do you do?"

"I count sheep."

"Does it work?"

"No."

"*Caramba!*"

"All night long!"

Ever since she had left the city she suffered from insomnia, and the eight or so hours a day set aside for resting were lost. And if in the best circumstances she managed to sleep she dreamt of useless things, lacking in reality and interest; of things she hadn't suggested, or desired, that were later forgotten, never again to come to mind, or if they did come back, they were nasty experiences because they arrived unexpectedly.

"I had a dream last night."

"Oh? What did you dream?"

"That I was being chased by cabbages disguised as lettuces."

"No!"

But it was better to plunge herself into the chaotic world and not lose sleep over it because the next day she might have an extra right foot, or she would grow a whole new leg and she'd have to learn how to walk with it, or the dark rings around her eyes would make her pupils seem hard and brittle. The light grated at her eyes, and she kept her eyelids closed in order to sink into shadow and not bump into things, into words, into ideas, dates, and relatives, confusing everything as if she had just been born and were carrying a mattress around on her back.

"What day is today?"

"What year is this?"

"Whose daughter am I?"

"What's my name?"

She lived the life that she had always wanted to lead, going from one place to another, seeking out countries, different people, ways of life leading to other topics she had never touched, feeling something unusual every daybreak, that time contained the only enigma that would never be solved, that what had been seen and felt yesterday wouldn't be seen and felt today or tomorrow. That the future was too ephemeral and that one life wasn't enough to touch, feel, and grab hold of so many things, so many bodies, so many illusions. She wanted to be thrust into all situations with all five senses, with some vital life force firmly rooted in her body, in order to witness the spectacle that was constantly being born, and which seemed to have been created at that very moment for herself alone, since she was the only one on the face of the earth who knew the secret of the sleeping city.

"I am."

"What?"

"Myself."

"Myself what . . . ?"

"I am now . . ."

"Now what?"

"I."

When she remembered her old family house, she couldn't erase the stains from her mind, the wet stains that seeped into the hotel's walls, making the primitive color of the paint stand out. There were water stains on the walls leading to the bathroom, and the water stains smelled of genuine sadness, that of knowing that one day all this had to end in a wild rush. For a moment it seemed as if the hotel room, with its high window, were Alvarito Catovil's room after the floor collapsed under the weight of the rug he had been weaving, leaving the window useless for looking out at the street. . . .

The old family house enclosed a whole world where Bruna's essence was scattered. It was worth remembering it year after year. Remembering the people who lived there, with all their spilled tears, and the quiet moments, which, as time went by, marked off the limits of their lives. Remembering them with all their illusions that no longer were illusions because they had become solid or had completely vanished into smoke. Remembering their heroic and ridiculous acts whose value was now inverted and different.

"Your grandfather was a very important man."

"Ah, rubbish!"

"What do you mean?"

"My grandfather was a jerk."

The house was filled with María Illacatu's sighs. The three-legged bench where that fool Alvarito sat to weave his rug . . . the huge pile of rusty swords that belonged to the bishop's sons . . . the rustic cedar box that held María the Twenty-third's gold pieces . . . the wobbly, hand-carved, finely brocaded wooden chairs where Camelia the Tearful's admirers sat . . . the pitcher of cane liquor for digging up the treasure . . . the first adding machine that arrived in the city . . . the bottle where they put the herb water made from *higuera negra* to counteract witchcraft. . . .

The problem of time tangled everything up; there was a lot of confusion about who were the grandparents and who were the grandchildren.

"Your grandfather was very rich."

"Don't you mean my great-great-grandfather?"

"I think so . . . I don't know. . . . I'm confused."

Bruna couldn't specify precisely how long they had really lived on the earth because, while some of them lived to reach one hundred years, in fact, they still had lullabies sung to them so they would sleep soundly.

"They say that Alvarito Catovil still made peepee in his bed until he was nearly seventy."

Others hadn't lived more than twenty years, but their hearts made them old, and they soon completed their time on the earth, paying dearly for the gift of life: their hearts pounded repeatedly and whirled around in such a way that by talking about them, their presence and prestige was kept up for generations and it seemed as if they were still alive.

"It seems like I can still see him with his little pointed beard and his walking stick."

"Who?"

"Your poor grandfather Francisco."

Some of the people who lived in the old family house had lived with such intensity that just eating a piece of bread was a whole story in itself: they put their five senses into this daily act and tasted the flour, the salt, the leavening, the warmth of the hands that had kneaded the dough, the temperature of the oven, the slap of the bread falling into the baker's basket. So much so that the others repeated these same simple and colorless acts all the days of their lives until they died. A few of the first ones began to doubt, which turned to a desperation that quickly led to hell, or they sat down with God to play a game of cards, shuffling the little pieces of their chopped-up souls.

"What a rotten life!"

"Quiet, don't tempt the Lord!"

"Any day now I'm going to shoot myself. . . ."

"Aaah! Don't blaspheme!"

Those who had defeated time in the sleeping city, and destroyed the clocks, and vanquished the absurd mechanism of conventions, and surpassed human possibilities without getting any satisfaction from it, were very few. They bore the mark of an unknown deity. Bruna was like them. She was descended from a race that should have disappeared along with their houses, their people, their prejudices, and their wrongheaded rituals.

"Your mother went to Mass every day. . . ."

"But not me."

"Your grandmother was a saint. . . ."

"Maybe, but not me."

"In my day that wasn't done. . . ."

"Well, I do it now."

1

Bruna's past was bound to three people, two great-aunts and a great-uncle, who lived in the old house. All three of them were stark raving mad, madness they in turn inherited from their ancestors.

"She's crazy."

"A chip off the old block."

"I never would have believed . . ."

"Much more than that . . . it runs in the family. . . ."

Among the shapeless mass of people who lived in the city, Bruna's ancestors stood out like scarecrows in a vegetable patch. It was a long line of maniacs. Aberrations and oddities nourished their lives and suffocated those who had to live alongside them. Many were considered important figures: treatises were written about their lives and works. But when they were passed through the sifter of truth and the crucible of time, when their actions were placed on perfectly honest scales, the needle didn't move. Laughter, tears, their shaky or secure steps on the earth, the pit-pat of their hearts, their words, looks, thoughts, all added up to nothing.

> *¿Qué se hizo el Rey Don Juan?*
> *Los infantes de Aragón,*
> *¿qué se hicieron . . . ?*

> What did the famous King Don Juan do?
> What did the children of Aragon do?

Bruna's old family house was joined to all the other houses that made up the city. The city had stayed asleep because they built it right where the winds changed direction, and they were still trying to free themselves from the influence of a sleep-inducing mountain sickness called *soroche*.

The people of the city took pills to prevent *soroche*, and when the pills ran out, the disease came back, making people sit and sit and sit, indefinitely. Indifference took them over, and they seized hold of the past because their hands were shaking and the past was what they could put their hands on most easily in their isolated state. They stopped feeling many sensations. Sluggishness came and sat on their knees, they let their arms fall to the earth until their fingers turned into roots, a hidden sadness gushed from their eyes, their breathing turned into broken sighs, and they fell into a comatose state when something new filtered in through the rain or the changing winds. They had fits of vertigo during which no one could find where they had left their heads or the little box where all their ideas and memories were kept.

"You know what?"

"What?"

"Nothing . . ."

" . . . !"

"Oh yes . . . But I don't remember anymore."

The differences between the city and what lay beyond the mountains cried out to be heard, but nobody listened. Sometimes the distance wasn't so great; an hour by plane was enough to reach another world. The city was unique. Surrounded by snowy mountains and strange vapors, it had made itself inaccessible. The imposition of a brutal and unbridled colonization, congenital sadness, the search for the box of ideas amid the old and moth-eaten junk in the attics, eyes that were always squinting in order to look backward, had turned the inhabitants of the city into headless beings. Nevertheless, they felt secure because they had been told that in other parts of the planet people were being driven crazy with so much rushing around. They said that Death was riding around on a motorcycle, hot on the mortals' heels.

"They say an electrically powered train derailed and took one thousand passengers with it."

"Sure! Over there! Who told them they could try to replace an engineer's brain with a spark plug? Those are the consequences of the sin of materialism. . . ."

2

Bruna was descended from a disloyal race that was still hurt and humiliated by its mixed blood with all the pain and repression of original sin.

"We don't have a drop of Indian blood."

"Neither do we."

"On the other hand . . . they do."

"All you have to do is look at the color of their faces."

"We all know each other here."

Bruna thought about the great majority of people who lived in the city and who silenced their ancestors if they didn't have an illustrious last name, a last name on top of which they could reconstruct according to their taste a brilliant past, whose foolish wisps were hammered into shape by means of a history forged during afternoon gatherings.

"Which Garcías are you related to?"

"The first ones to come to America."

"Which ones?"

"The founders, of course."

"The family of García Moreno?"

"Yes, exactly, the very same! Our great-grandfather was married to . . ."

Bruna's own relatives were ashamed of their crazy uncles and tried to lessen their manias with stories that changed meaning and circumstances, depending on the taste of each generation, as if the dead were the bitter fruit of the living. There was an uncomfortable silence on the subject of the ancestors' faults, even though these were so obvious that they had been recorded in the pages of a book and, even worse, in the minds of a whole generation.

"Who was this one?"

"A relative, I think."

"My great-uncle? The loony with the matches?"

"He was a very, very distant relative, practically not a relative at all."

The violence, betrayals, and stormy episodes wounded the sensibility of the living, who had to carry the imaginary baggage of the supposed sins of the dead. They made unheard-of efforts to provide for the humble and poor a rank and lineage that they had never had, or dreamed of having, because perhaps in life it would have weighed on them like a burden too heavy for their shoulders.

"Did my grandfather really dig potatoes?"

"Ridiculous! The Indians on his hacienda did that."

"What hacienda?"

"One . . . that he had."

"Where?"

"Oh, that way. . . ."

They quickly hid the yellowing daguerreotypes that showed a piece of the family tree dressed in a miserable outfit that was a sign of poverty, or mocking them with the unerasable features of the damned race.

"Who is this a picture of?"

"I don't know. Maybe one of the servants. . . ."

"But here's our family name. . . ."

"Oh yes? Then it's your grandfather. But he's dressed in a costume for Innocents' Day."

"He looks like an Indian. . . ."

"No, he was very white. He's wearing makeup here. . . . In those days people knew how to have more fun than we do today."

"Let me keep this photo of my grandfather!"

"No, no, that's impossible! Put it back!"

However, they didn't have the nerve to destroy the old piece of cardboard because a superstitious fear kept them from doing it. An invisible hand had changed the grandfather's nose into theirs, and they were afraid that if they ripped up the photo, their own noses would bleed amid the offal in the garbage. For this reason they kept the photo at the back of the wardrobe chest, under lock and key, but afraid that at any moment the tattered grandfather would come to life and would come out at the most inopportune time like a bad dream, or improper thoughts, to tell the truth about a last name, or a date, or else to reclaim his nose. Until finally one day, armed with an unheard-of bravery, they tore up the photo into a thousand pieces and felt liberated, and acquired as if by magic the rank and prestige that they had so desperately been desiring.

The children waited breathlessly for a moment when nobody was watching in order to open the closet and liberate the dusty grandfather who, from the distant exile of his dishonor, smiled at them and told them stories and truths about the times and about noses. But the children grew, and as soon as they learned the meaning of the words "family name" they gave the wardrobe key another turn and forgot about the grandfather.

Bruna laughed at those who made a show of having an illustrious family name that hadn't come down through the normal pathways of having to "go forth and multiply," but rather through the tortuous and degenerated tales of the grandfather who was a bishop. But since the grandfather had come from good lineage, nobody was ashamed of his mistakes, and since the dates were reversed, the result was always the same: the grandfather became a widower of a nonexistent dead woman and in order to beg for the eternal rest of the nonexistent dead woman's soul, he became a bishop overnight, with the knowledge and consent of the present and future generations.

"And if he was a bishop, how did he have kids? . . ."

"That was before, many years before. He had the heroism to vanquish worldly pleasures and to devote himself to God."

All the inhabitants of the city had a family tree; they took great pleasure in pruning and watering it every afternoon. One time, one of them found a bird among the branches of the tree. The bird had a noble title and he accepted it gladly, and ever since then he has put its eggshell in the coat of arms over the door of his ancestral home (homes, in order to be homes, must be ancestral). But when an Indian appeared wearing a poncho and hemp sandals, even though the Indian was endowed with valor, loyalty, manliness, they pruned that branch of the tree and the Indian fell to the ground to be used as fertilizer.

"Your name is Juan Espejo! You wouldn't be, perhaps, a descendant of one of our greatest men: Eugenio Espejo . . . ?"

"No, never! That Espejo was an Indian, and his name was Chugshi. He stole that name. We are from the . . ."

Bruna, scandalizing her relatives, who thought she was crazy, signed her name with the original family name of her Indian grandmother. Her attitude, more than mere impudence, sprang from what she remembered of the city's history and had discovered of her family's history, and it seemed to her puerile and absurd to cover up with such a conventional lie the truth that was there for anybody to see, anybody who, like her, had taken a walk around the silent and surprising pathways of the archives.

"Where did you get this Illacatu from? . . ."

"From the archives. I know that I'm an Illacatu and not a Catovil."

The story of her last name was a very common story in those days. . . . A man from the other side of the ocean, thirsty for adventures and gold—because those men were the ones who actually did the colonizing, helped along by some laws that fell into the sea and sank—this man had married an Indian. She was the daughter of a chief who owned mountains of gold and emeralds. The white man saw the sky brighten. . . . Men such as he forged and fed the legend of El Dorado for centuries and spread it around the world, reawakening a form of greed that had been latent since the days of Ali Baba. The Indian's name was María Illacatu.

"I baptize you, Yahuma, with the name María. In the name of the Father, the Son, and the . . ."

And she was named María from the moment they spilled water over her bowed head and washed away the idea of the sun god, chilling her heart, which had been warmed by the fire of his rays, and told her about some unknown god who seemed to get angry much more often than he should have.

"Idol worshiper! God will punish you! You're going to go to hell! You're going to be condemned!"

". . . ?"

Little by little they created two opposing voices in her ears that left her deaf to the words that can be heard even though no lips have spoken them. María Illacatu stopped hearing the voices that speak in the shadows, in a smile, in a suppressed cry, among the leaves of corn, in the depths of someone's eyes. She remained alone, in a solitude filled with questions without answers that rose up with the firmness of snakes coiled for attack. In a solitude plagued with desperate cries that died without leaving an echo and that grated at the skin like the chirping of crickets.

"Hail Mary, full with grace, Lord with thee, thy womb Jesus. Amen."

"Father who is apart in Heaven with thy name. Give us bread every day. Do thy will. Daily bread. Forgive the sins of our death amen."

María Illacatu's children were much more their father's children than their mother's. They were aware how much prestige the so easily gotten gold brought them, and they changed their innocuous name García to Villacatu.

"Here in Spain everyone's García. . . ."

"It's a noble name. . . ."

"Our name is Villacatu. Our mother was of royal blood."

They grew up in their father's land, in a tiny village, and the fact that they were Spanish American surrounded them with a halo of dignity that accompanied them even in their most private and ordinary acts.

Their children grew up in their mother's land and therefore cursed the day that their fathers changed their name. In the land they were living everything was still waiting to be made, so they adopted the name of Villa-Cató, and in turn, the children of the Villa-Catós settled the long-debated question of lineage by calling themselves Catovil.

"Villacatu is Indian, pure Quichua. . . ."

"We own six villas."

"Villa-Cató doesn't sound bad!"

"Catovil sounds better!"

"That's it! What a relief to be rid of that Villacatu!"

That's how all reference to the Indian grandmother was lost, until Bruna came into the world of her own life, holding old Mama Chana's hand; years later, in the terrible and unsuspected world of the archives, where the erasures and uprootings were so brazenly done, these were the first things she saw when the dusty books were opened.

"Here are the papers. Be careful. They're crumbling. Time and humidity . . ."

Bruna was shaken by the discovery of her true roots; she wasn't the child of her parents, or the grandchild of her grandparents, or the niece of her aunts and uncles. She was a being floating in air.

"Finally! I found what I've been looking for. . . ."

"What, señorita?"

"Something about my ancestors. . . ."

"Many people come here searching for that."

"A name's been scratched out . . . and another one's written over it, in different handwriting and different ink!"

"Yes, it's true. The emendation was made much, much later."

"Maybe after a century?"

"Maybe, maybe. . . ."

Ever since she wrote her first name next to the last name that was really hers, she felt her feet fall more firmly on the earth. That she wasn't a wild bird flying along the ground, like a leaf fallen from some tree, but a concrete being. She discovered the reason for her secret rebellions and charted her own course like the sole captain of her own ship: she could have a family tree and yet forget that she had one. She could lie down to sleep in its shade without the leaves falling on her or the branches giving way. It was a tree nourished with blood, and at the same time, she was the uppermost branch.

"I've got Indian blood!"

"Are you crazy? . . ."

"Mama Chana told me that. . . ."

"I've told you not to speak to the servants."

"I saw in the archives that my great-great-grandmother was an Indian. . . ."

"Jesus! What a crazy thing to say!"

Bruna's family preserved like a treasure—without knowing who it was—a painting of the Indian grandmother. She was dressed like a great lady as a result of her unfortunate marriage. The man who did the portrait painted her as she was. But influenced by the conventions of the era, he removed her skin, and thus flayed, he gave her living flesh the skin her husband lent her so she could pose. María Illacatu lost her coppery skin on the canvas with the same stoicism with which she lost her reason for living. Her face, her neck, and her arms were all milky white, unreal, as if they had undergone plastic surgery, like the new skin transplants that were now arriving in the city. She was the image of what they wished she had been.

"This is your great-great-grandmother. . . ."

"That's a lie! My great-great-grandmother was an Indian!"

"But can't you see that she's not an Indian?"

"Then it's not her. . . ."

The man who painted the portrait was an extraordinary artist; he re-created the model's pain and melancholy on canvas. She had a superhuman expression: a bluish gray tint surrounded the figure, giving it a solitary look against this background, as if she were a being transported from somewhere else. She looked as if she were alone on the earth, abandoned by all, guardian of her own pain, lookout post of her limitless amazement, rooted to the spot like a bolt of wonder that the sun god might have cast down from above. In her Oriental eyes one could see the massacre of an entire civilization, whose best accomplishments were torn out by the roots and forsaken and whose vices were perfected so that they could be dominated without remorse.

"My great-great-grandmother looks sad. . . ."

"But she looks very elegant."

"It looks like she's about to cry. . . ."

"Nonsense! Back then the women didn't have the romantic affectations of today's women."

Her left hand softly leaning on the back of a chair, which looked like a useless piece of furniture, fooled the spectator who was unfamiliar with the Indian woman's history. Her hand held a half-open fan that looked more like a weapon from the way she gripped it. The fan in her hands was so absurd that, in spite of seeing what it was, people had to ask what she was holding. The bluish veins of her right fist displayed the concealed rebellion, the powerful audacity, of someone who was practically a child because of her age and the neglect in which they made her live. She was small and delicate, like an exotic plant transplanted to a luxurious garden and kept alive with vitamins.

"Isn't it true, Mama Chana, that my grandmother looks like she's about to hit someone with her fan?"

"Yes, child, yes, she would have liked to hit her shameless husband."

"My grandfather? Why, was he bad?"

"He was perverse. . . . Quiet, quiet, your aunts can hear. . . ."

María Illacatu had succumbed long before they made the portrait. She didn't resist the tragic process of being transplanted and adapting to the world of the whites. Her centuries-old customs, inherited along with the earth by racial privilege, were supposed to have been erased overnight as if they were stigmas.

"We have to put a corset on the Indian so she can pose."

"And you're going to spend so much money getting her picture painted?"

"So that my grandchildren won't say that—"

"Oh, now I understand!"

María Illacatu's thoughts had to change course, producing a bombardment of ideas in her brain that destroyed her words, and go from simplicity to chaos. Her feelings had to come undone like old clothing. She had to wash her heart in brine until love turned into hate. And she had to make all these changes in order to live through the misery of daily existence and had to do it without understanding why, without any explanation. . . .

"The Indian is pretty, but stupid."

"She has to be tamed like a wild mare. She has to get used to slippers and silk stockings."

No hand reached out to help her walk toward the emptiness; she had to do it all by her own strength, without knowing how, or why, or for what.

"You can't be loving with them, because they're Indians."

"You have to be hard with them, so they'll learn."

It was an infinitely difficult adaptation, almost superhuman, that only the inept and servile managed to complete.

"El Puma doesn't want to be forced to be a servant."

"Whip him until he does want to!"

"Amaluisa has escaped!"

"Hunt him down with dogs!"

An impossible adaptation that would last for centuries, resulting in generations of beings who would live here and there, like wisps of straw, and that won't be erased from the face of the earth until the last native refuses to cover his feet, own one set of clothes for work and another for rest, eat bread without the acidic taste of sweat, feel happiness when he wakes up in the morning, and gets an answer to the questions that sprout up like thistles in the narrow horizon of his darkest thoughts.

María Illacatu was an adorable child pressed between two cultures that didn't even fight between themselves, because they never knew anything about each other.

"The Indians over there. The whites over here."

Sometimes even they got stuck at the crossroads, in massacres and ambushes, with their mouths open, because they didn't know whether to kill the enemy or pound their heads against the rocks in order to kill the ideas they had inside, which were the cause of their acts and the reason they took up the harquebus, the knife, the sword, the club . . .

María Illacatu died a few years before the local nobles who envied her beauty and wealth killed her with their curious glances. She died the very same day that a group of adventurers from beyond the mountains and the ocean found her while looking for the trail to the city of El Dorado.

A group of bearded men with swords, shields, and hearts of steel were wandering lost among the precipices and canyons of a place that they could neither enter nor leave because a demon took delight in pushing them toward the heart of the mountains. The heart of the mountains was the last defense of the Indian chief who was waiting for the end to come, squatting on the pain of recent events. The chief had a daughter who was going to marry the sun god. But when the adventurers found her, the sun was eclipsed and María Illacatu left her soul hanging from the top of the highest tree. Her eyes remained fixed on the darkness that covered the sky, and because she was blind she allowed herself to be led by he who would become her master and her executioner toward the fog that enveloped a faraway city.

A team of llamas loaded with gold and emeralds marked María Illacatu's path along canyons that were never seen again, never visited by any human being. As the shadow of the *ñusta* passed by with her jailers, her Indian brothers went and cut all the ropes that held up the swaying reed bridges with the same savage fury with which hopeless people slit their pulsing veins. They blocked the narrow roads with huge boulders that they rolled off the summits so that the evil spirits would never come back and so that the hunting party would disappear into the decaying vegetable matter and the earth's rocky entrails. But they would never forget the beautiful young girl's tears as she was stolen by the foreigners.

It was a voyage toward death. The road kept growing longer, as if it were made of rubber. It went through the mountains, inventing curves that hadn't existed before, passing three or four times over the same places. They went along, rising and falling from summit to abyss, confusing the clouds with the rushing water of the rivers.

Bitten by the cold, nauseated by the heat, the caravan went along, feeding generations of mosquitoes that got drunk on the taste of the unfamiliar blood. The bones of men and animals were left to bleach on the road and were picked clean by the buzzards' ruthless beaks. They went along making prayers to the rocks and scattering curses into the air.

And they would have gone on walking for centuries and centuries if María Illacatu hadn't felt a cyclone growing in her belly that was destined to come into the world transformed into a human being, with one white arm and one Indian arm, with one leg of a *chasqui* messenger and another of a nobleman's son, with a heart that made rhythmic mistakes because the blood flowed or curdled within the astonished veins, with one eye as light as a corn kernel and the other as dark as wheat.

"The Indian's going into labor!"

"It doesn't matter . . . we're almost there."

"The captain doesn't want us to say 'Indian.'. . ."

María Illacatu told the road of her secret maternity, and the road had pity on her and suddenly grew shorter, ending on the commons

24

of a city that opened its windows to see the caravan arriving. Nobody noticed how the earth slipped into the ravines and the mountains drew back. The road shrank: ten trees became one. Birds fell dead from old age, and the eggs that they had just laid grew wings. María Illacatu saw the sleeping city and was not amazed, because her ability to be amazed had stayed behind with her soul, which she had left hanging from the branches of a tree.

She learned the whites' language, but she refused to speak it; the words born in her throat had a different meaning. When she sensed that she was the target of the city dwellers' looks, she felt such a sensation of contempt—as if a thousand shoes were trampling on her face—and in spite of the fact that she knew the meaning of the new words, she never spoke them: it was a small compensation. . . .

"Don't say *huasi,* say 'ho-o-use.' Don't say *alpa,* say 'e-e-earth.' Don't say *rumi,* say 'sto-o-one.' Don't say *cari,* say 'ma-a-an.' Don't say *huarmi,* say 'wo-man.' Don't say *tanda,* say 'bread.' Don't say *ashcu,* say 'do-o-og.' Don't say *misi,* say 'ca-a-at.' Don't say, don't say, don't say . . ."

While the husband was building the three-story house, she spent hours sitting in the garden, in the shadow of an uprooted memory, looking into the dark bottom of the well, where she always believed she saw a friendly face. Later her descendants would confuse that face with the malign reflection of the eye of the Devil.

Little by little, having children reconciled her to her painful existence. She found a reason for being there, in that house. But a wall of silence had grown up between her and the white man, behind which the laughter and scorn of the white people fell upon her like stones; she reacted by closing herself in her shell, refusing to use a fork to bring food to her mouth, resisting all the new things that had been imposed on her to learn. She remained impermeable to certain acts that struck her as absurd rites, such as how to handle a fan in order to dispel a flush of color, or to sit in front of a stretching frame, inserting and removing the needle in order to render in cloth some flowers that were as imprisoned as she was, or to con-

25

verse about the insipid everyday occurrences in the sleeping city at the long evening parties at which she had to present herself, so that all the guests could see her, dressed in the same style as the other women. During the gatherings she didn't say one word or make a single movement when she felt she was being talked about. She managed to keep her blood calm under her skin and her muscles as tense as if they were made of wood. Which was why those present thought that María Illacatu was a beautiful example of stupidity into which the light of intelligence had not penetrated and that it was impossible for her to notice the sideways glances or the pauses directed at her in the cruel jokes that made her bleed inside.

"Go ahead and talk, she doesn't understand our language."

"Indians are naturally stupid. The language of Castile wasn't made for them."

"She's a pure-blooded horse."

"Wrong, she's a mare!"

"Ha, ha, ha . . ."

The husband, made rich by the *ñusta*'s gold, kept her by his side until he crossed the ocean again to spread the legends of the Spanish Americans who found treasures wherever they went. He didn't bring the woman because she weighed too much. No ship had room for her and her pain; she and her solitude were rooted to the earth.

But he drained all of María Illacatu's blood when he took her children away. Those children for whose sake one afternoon she sent a bird to go looking for her soul, which she had left hanging on a branch of the tallest tree near her old home.

When she kissed her children good-bye, she put a piece of her newly arrived soul under each of their shirts. When the ship that had taken them away was on the high sea, the children took off their shirts, and the pieces of María Illacatu's soul flew back up and attached themselves to the points of the stars, unable to reunite until much later. They stayed there, fluttering like kerchiefs, saying good-bye to all the children in the world.

"Good-bye, Mama. . . . Your blessing!"

"She's not your mother, she's an Indian. . . ."

"I don't care! I love her. . . . And she loves me, too. . . ."

"I don't want any tears! Let's go!"

When the husband came back, he didn't bring the children. He left them in the care of their paternal grandparents. In his baggage he brought a royal commission, hams, bacon, garlic sausages, and a nobleman's coat of arms done on parchment. When the man and the woman met again, she looked at him for the first time in her life: the white man was the strangest and most detestable being in all of her bad dreams and nightmares. This time she didn't say a word, either.

". . . ?"

"I left them there, in Spain."

". . . ?"

"So they can be educated."

". . . !"

One night when the white man came back from his gallivanting with a local woman who was old and ugly but from a noble family, and whom he had decided to marry—pending the dispensation from the pope and those who were still debating among themselves whether or not Indians had souls—María Illacatu sent the bird to bring back her eyes, which had been lost in the darkness of the eclipse; and when the bird came back with her eyes, she put them back in: that instant the furniture changed position, the white people shrank in stature, she saw the things that were inside the baggage, saw that her children had lost what she had put under their shirts, and she waited. . . .

With her own eyes in place, that night would also be the last night that she would dance her native dances nude to the sound of an out-of-tune guitar that was writhing in pain, to the rhythm of a braided leather whip with which she was habitually beaten. It was the last time that she would see the white man sleep, satiated with liquor and pleasure. . . . She opened for the first time the large sewing kit that someone had given her as a present and, after taking

27

out some thin, sharp scissors, she plunged them into the man's heart. . . .

The scissors remained still for a moment, feeling the warm blood: they experimented with the pleasure of penetrating a warm, moist, living being and then, drunk with lust and pleasure, started all by themselves to cut and cut the stretched-out body, as if it were some kind of macabre game. . . .

It was two in the morning; the candle had burned out, tired of crying huge wax tears onto the silver candelabra. The bloody pieces of the man wriggled around on the floor, trying to rejoin, but in spite of their desperate efforts, they couldn't do it. The arms were rejected by the groin, the legs slipped away from the shoulders, the head couldn't join with the belly, the eyes slid along the back. María Illacatu washed her blood-red hands, slowly started to undo her braids, and . . . she hung herself with her own hair. . . .

The scissors kept cutting and cutting until somebody wrenched them from what had long since been a cadaver. Then they jumped out the window and into the street and started to cut up the rocks, the tree trunks, the river water, and stopped only when they started to shear the wool off the sheep who would become the mothers of those sheep who, a century later, would have to give their wool to one of María Illacatu's descendants so that he could start weaving the largest carpet in the world.

When María Illacatu's children became men thanks to the work-ings of clocks and biology, they decided unanimously in a family meeting on the change from García to Villacatu, and then they returned to the land of gold. They hushed up the rumors sur-rounding their parents' deaths, one of whom—it was said—died of heart prostration and the other of puerperal fever, until they fully convinced themselves that that was the reality. . . .

Once installed in the city, which they did not remember very well, they had the disagreeable surprise of finding that there weren't any more rich Indians for them to marry and later repudiate. What they found were women who knew how to handle a fork and raise their little fingers when drinking tea. How to paint snowy landscapes that they had never seen. How to go to Mass every day with an Indian servant girl carrying the kneeling bench on her back through the cobblestone streets, while older ones showed their devotion by kneeling on large silk pillows that they also sat on to listen to long sermons in which they discussed and condemned the sins of the flesh, called the Devil all kinds of names, and begged for clemency for a corrupt world. . . . The women of the city also knew how to handle a fan, behind which they practiced their first, incipient lessons in coquetry. They urinated between five and six times a day in golden chamber pots and spent the rest of the day yawning and dreaming of marrying a noble, rich, and elegant gentleman. They were completely the opposite of what their unknown mother had been.

Once they possessed the riches inherited from their mother's side and the noble title bought by their father's side, the Villacatus remained single for a very short time. The women's fans went into action, and little perfumed notes came and went, carried next to the breasts of eager, older maids and under the very eyes of the respective fathers, who, long beforehand, had been chattering about how the children should marry. . . .

Nobody ever heard about María Illacatu again, because by mutual agreement they took her and buried her in the box with the dusty memories, from which she would never escape.

It always hurt Bruna to see her Indian ancestor nailed up in the big drawing room, isolated from all contact and tenderness by a wall of silence and mistaken words. Nobody seemed to know anything about her past, and if they kept the painting in an honored place in the house, it was because a superstitious fear kept them from touching or even getting near it. It was said that on moonlit nights, when the rays penetrated through the cracks in the closed windows, sighs and laments could be heard that froze the blood.

There was another truth: the painting was a valuable work of art. The signature that the artist put in the lower right corner had acquired fame with the passing of the years.

When Bruna discovered on her own and through Mama Chana's delicious indiscretions the scandal surrounding her distant relatives, she started to venerate her Indian grandmother. She wanted to take the large painting and hang it at the head of her bed to remove her grandmother from memory and give her the warmth that she never had in life. But it was too late now. She was no longer her grandmother. In reality, she never had the slightest relationship with the people who lived in the house. With the passing of time it just became a valuable painting, with an astonishing resemblance to a Bonnat, which depicted a great lady from the other side of the ocean and nothing else. . . .

"Who's that?"

"One of our ancestors."

"She's so beautiful!"

"The painting is very valuable, it's been appraised at—"

"How distinguished!"

"Of course, she had noble titles!"

3

Bruna's family house, built by an adventurer who engendered the most absurd offspring, was an enormous, rambling house full of byways and symmetrically placed windows that made it look like a convent. The facade had half columns of bluish stone, and over the main entrance was a coat of arms with castles, huge ugly birds, and diagonal lines. The tiles were nearly vertical on the high-peaked roof, so the water could pour off in two directions. There was a very large oak door that was opened only on important occasions. Ordinarily the house's inhabitants used a small false door, ensconced in the right-hand side of the big door, like its child. The small door had a small window for examining the sex, the social status, the age, and the thoughts of the people who wanted to be let in.

"Knock-knock-knock."

"Who is it?"

"Don Martín Pérez de la Perinola."

"Open the big doors and the drawing-room windows."

"Knock-knock-knock."

"Who is it?"

"Bless be God, master. . . ."

"Open the small door and tell him to wash his feet."

It had a long, dark entranceway with finely inlaid bull vertebras that, at night, rearranged themselves trying to find each other. The bones wanted to rejoin to form a spinal column that would resurrect the whole animal. At night strange noises could be heard, and when the morning came the vertebras were found in great disorder, forming a cabalistic mosaic of swearwords and obscene figures that the children of the house didn't understand and, thinking they were puzzles, tried to put back together; but they never could because the pieces were so strongly adhered to the earth with a mortar of clay, wood shavings, and bull's blood.

"Let's go to the front entrance!"

"Yes, let's go see the bones!"

"See? This wasn't here before. . . . Nor this . . . nor this. . . ."

"These are the most magical bones I've ever seen!"

The house had been built taking advantage of the unevenness of the ground leading up to the foot of the cold, craggy mountain. It had three floors on the main street, two on the side street, and only one floor on the other side and behind.

There was an orchard in back with an alley of lemon trees and a very tall, hundred-year-old cherry tree that dropped its fruit all over the orchard and onto the neighbors' patios and whose branches sheltered hundreds of skittish and gluttonous singing birds. And there was a well with the eye of the Devil in the bottom. This eye of the Devil could see inside people's heads, see into the thoughts that they were forming, and could scream out loud the sins of the people who leaned over its mouth, for all to know. That was why nobody looked into its dark bottom.

"Don't go near the well: the Devil's in there."

"We're just going to look at it from far away."

"I said no. The Devil will get you."

"We're going to throw rocks at it. . . ."

"No, the eye is watching you!"

Fear restrained even the curiosity of the children, who felt guilty without having sinned because they lived in an atmosphere in which evil was almighty. Evil filled all the spaces; it filled the hollows of the hands, the tiny holes near the tear ducts, it lodged between the tongue and palate, behind doors, under sheets, in empty bottles, in locked closets. Only María Illacatu in her moments of anguish, when solitude clawed at her feeble ribs, looked into the well's bottom and saw herself transported to the center of the earth, finding a good friend in the enormous pupil that shined beyond the water and her tears.

The house had steps, slopes, and greenery all over. It was a neighborhood unto itself, where dull-witted people lived, oblivious of their intimacy with echoes and gloom. They lay down to rest on straw mattresses that were kept in the attic, conceiving over the years thousands of little ghosts who took over the house and learned how to walk, like flesh-and-blood children, grabbing on to the dining room's grillework before they took their first steps.

"Do you hear those noises? Are they mice?"

"No, mice don't sound like that. . . ."

"Then . . . ? What are they?"

"Shhhh, they're ghosts!"

The main bedrooms opened onto the patio. The patio was surrounded on all four sides with long, wide corridors, with rustic wooden floors that were washed the first Friday of every month with a mixture of creosote and water. The wooden railings were painted the bright green color of grass. Most of the bedrooms had their own doors and windows, except for the rooms that adjoined the neighboring house. When it rained, the doors that opened onto the patio were closed and the rooms connected to each other by means of inner doors; some furniture was moved away, and one could walk the length of the house. While the desolate rain fell, the old women started praying the rosary and burning holy rosemary, and the children, who were always in the house, took advantage of the disorder of the displaced furniture to play hide-and-seek under the beds and inside the big closets.

There was a large fountain in the middle of the patio, almost one meter in diameter, made out of a single block of stone fitted on top of a column that was twisted like a honey cake. Surrounding this, a large polygon received the water that poured down from above.

The fountain's central decoration was changed many times

according to the taste of the homeowners; the fountain was a reflection of its inhabitants. At first there was just a basin into which the water glided peacefully. When Camelia the Tearful lived in the house, she commissioned a large bronze figure that depicted a graceful little mermaid holding up a conch shell. During the time of Aunt Catalina—*caca de gallina*—the little mermaid was replaced by a voluminous stone fish with water pouring pointlessly from its wide-open mouth. The expression on the fish's face was absurd and stupid.

"The fish in the fountain looks like dumb Manuei, it looks like an idiot."

"Don't say that again! The fish is the symbol of the first Christians."

"And why did the first Christians go around with their mouths open, huh?"

When Camelia the Tearful died, Aunt Catalina ordered them to remove the little mermaid that brought Hans Christian Andersen's fairy tale to mind, because she alleged that it was nude. The little mermaid was removed and taken to back rooms of the house, the ones near the orchard, where she died of cold and sorrow.

"I've given orders to remove that naked woman from the fountain!"

"Mama Chana! Make some clothes for the little mermaid, so they won't remove her from the fountain!"

When Aunt Catalina died, exuding odors of complete sanctity, the fish was replaced by a stone "pisstatue," almost life-size, that was brought with great effort by Bruna's brother, the one who crossed the whole of Europe chasing after a ballerina's pretty legs.

"I hate that fish! I've always hated it!"

"Our great-aunt said that it was from the first Christians. . . ."

"Ridiculous! I'm going to get rid of it. I've brought a 'pisstatue.'"

"Who is it?"

"A little prince who wandered from his palace, got lost, and when they found him, he looked like this. . . ."

"Ahhh! With his *pipí* sticking up?"

The patio's blend of colors brought back memories of something out of fairy tales and lullabies. There were large standing flower pots full of geraniums everywhere. Little trails of grass were trying to survive in the tiny spaces between the flagstones, and there was something heartwarming about them, their eagerness to survive, their generous goal of outlining the forms of the gray stones in the monotonous, peaceful patio. . . .

They hung some canary cages from the beams on the second-floor balcony; the birds sang, sprinkling the silence with yellow daisies from their throats.

Enormous Angora cats went wherever they felt like going and left the same way, which was why the corridors were scrubbed with creosote the first Friday of every month.

Comfortable wicker chairs in the corners of the patio invited one to sit on them and watch the water falling from the fountain.

The water from the fountain had its own special language for each member of the old house: for María Illacatu it was an unrestrainable flood of tears. When she watched the water, she thought: I cry more than the fountain, my tears can't be seen, but they will never, never dry up. . . .

For the woman who married one of her sons, and who was insufferably sanctimonious, the water from the fountain was a stream of Hail Marys; she sat in front of it for thirty years, waiting for a shooting star to fall that would either save her or condemn her.

"Glu-glu-glu-glu."

"I'm saved—I'm condemned—I'm saved—I'm condemned . . ."

In the time of the little mermaid, Camelia the Tearful and her cortege of admirers went into raptures over the feminine shapes, and the one who succeeded in becoming her husband composed the most obvious sonnet about the first Eve coming out of the depths of the sea.

Pearly creature of rounded forms.
Neptune gives you a kiss.
The fleecy mother-of-pearl . . .

Alvarito de Villa-Cató submerged his burning hands in the water from the fountain to reduce the swelling from the constant friction of the woolen threads with which he was weaving his carpet.

"My hands are burning!"

"Of course, you never rest!"

"I can't! I don't have the time!"

The bishop of Villa-Cató conceived his audacious plan while watching the water from the fountain; María the Twenty-third got into it whenever she felt like it. Aunt Clarita took water from the fountain every afternoon to water her geraniums. Bruna and her siblings made little paper boats, set to sea in them, and sailed far away from the *soroche* that still held the sleeping city, while the "pis-statue" listened to the sound of the spiders spinning their shapeless webs.

4

When they all lived together in the house, Bruna went through her childhood and her first rebellions surrounded by her family. It wasn't a very sumptuous house by then. The man who married the Indian grandmother did nothing to increase the fortune, and those who came after dedicated themselves to spending what was left on the most outrageous enterprises. But it was a big, happy, sun-filled house. Only toward the end of the day did one feel a slight uneasiness, as if the previous generations were present, with their eyes fixed on the back of one's head.

"I feel like someone's watching me. . . ."

"The same thing happens to me when I'm alone. . . ."

Everything in this house was preserved: the vices, the manias, the sorrows, and the tasteless pleasures. They guessed that everyone who once lived within its walls had left behind nothing more than family history and was anxiously awaiting reincarnation in order to live again, more deeply this time. But for Bruna, the old family house was the sweetest, most welcoming spot on earth, she always wanted to go back to it in search of life's essence and vitality. Whenever she felt like returning to the city, she felt a craving for the old family house, and only then could she go inside herself in search of peace.

"If I were back in the house, I'd be able to organize my thoughts."

"I know just what I'd do . . . I'd sit near the fountain and sun-bathe."

All of Bruna's ancestors were there, she knew each one of them, and she didn't feel strange when the presence of the past became so visible. She knew that they had to die to make way for the others, and that many of them died while they were still alive and even took a fancy to celebrating their own funerals.

Unfortunately, one generation had to eliminate the next, because even though the world had room for all, there were opportunities for only a few. Civilization wasn't advanced enough to yield, with elegance and nobility, to those who trampled on its heels looking for the best place for themselves to live. The world was topsy-turvy, as if God had built a lunatic asylum where nobody stayed where they belonged. The old ones kept expanding their spheres of influence and kept monopolizing the vital living space of those who lived under their dominion.

"I'm your father, and you must respect me!"

"I'm your mother, and you must obey me!"

"I'm your boss, and you must discuss everything you do with me!"

"I'm your confessor, and you must tell me your most secret thoughts!"

They didn't see that nobody yielded to anyone, because they were living only half a life, yet they still wanted to enjoy even those bits and pieces of lives and living spaces that weren't theirs. They were bottomless barrels, incapable of holding on to anything for themselves or for others. They lived a plantlike existence, and when they realized that their chlorophyll was running out they anxiously wanted to start over, and when they started over they felt more secure and once more let the days go by without being aware of the fact that time never goes backward. They started vegetating again, without making use of their time, without love, like puppets worked by the strings of circumstances, of customs, of chance occurrences that almost always tied them up in impossible knots, causing spiritual ailments, without thinking that the solutions could be found by drinking in the thoughts of others, if only for an instant.

Bruna lived each moment with intensity because she knew that she had to retreat, to stand gallantly to one side, so as not to interfere with someone else's sphere of life and so that hers wouldn't be invaded by intruders. She had to make absolute order out of her daily spiritual relations, something like the system of street traffic control. Seeing the disorder and abuses in men's relations, Bruna often repeated, so as to convince herself:

"When I'm older I'll do what I have to do, which is the hardest thing in the world. When I'm a mother, I'll be my children's friend only. When I'm a grandmother, I will tell my children's children stories without comparing their actions with mine at their age. I will never interfere with anybody's sphere of life. . . ."

Full of life and feeling her own emotions, she would watch others pass by, but—ah, yes—with a sardonic smile, seeing their hurry to get nowhere. Nobody could take away her right to laugh at the people passing by with all their useless baggage, full of candy wrappers, parchments, stuffed animals, little grudges that fit in the spaces between their teeth and yet weighed tons, envies folded up in yellow paper, washbasins, gold pieces that, at the end of the trip, wouldn't even buy a tear and were the burden of a completely useless existence because they took up so much space that there wasn't any room left for anybody, or anything. . . . It would have been better if all of them had remained within the uterine cycle.

It would be difficult for her grandchildren, if she ever managed to have any, if the name Catovil, or better said Illacatu, didn't die with her; but maybe they wouldn't have to age as quickly as she did.

The sight of some huge, ugly birds that traveled with her on one of her frequent escapes from the sleeping city spurred her on with her projects for the future. They were, in fact, some women dressed in see-through, violent-colored nightgowns, covered with glass beads and ribbons, in the fashion of the young rebels whose feelings and rebellions they had never experienced; half-naked, flabby, plump, painted, as if they lived in a never-ending carnival, fighting desperately against time and good taste, to seize, in the tropical air, a few last sparks of a youth lost forever.

When the women got off the boat that carried them to the youthful paradise, they screeched like magpies, they waddled like seals, they were barrels of rancid fat trying to compete with the svelte natives of an island in the ocean.

"Señores tourists: bathe in the Bahamas' fountain of youth. Time does not pass on the sunny beaches. Recover your youth on the miraculous sands of these enchanting beaches."

No, that wasn't youth, something on the surface of pinkish skin, hormones and surgery, firm, hard flesh, the absence of wrinkles on the face, where time sows and incubates its seeds; youth was an open and sincere approach to life, the ability to fall in love with someone or something, an inner power to daydream, a tendency toward love and understanding, a vitality for friendship, and an energy for getting through daily life. There would always be the eternal problem of the spirit, never of the body, and of the balance between being and *Being*. . . .

5

When María Illacatu's children came back, one of them set his eyes on a local woman of high birth, good for absolutely nothing, very white, very stupid, and very pious. She had been born with the condition of a very small brain. She had absorbed by osmosis all the prejudices and conventions that reigned in the sleeping city, as well as the vapors of *soroche*.

Obsessed by the weight of nobility, which was no longer over their entranceway but in their heads, María Illacatu's oldest son and the pious woman complemented each other perfectly, joining in a marriage infested with children, whispers, and prayers, in which they spent a lifetime minding appearances, the blueness of blood, and good manners.

"One drinks hot chocolate with the little finger raised and with small sips, so as not to make any noise. A gentleman must open doors for a lady. Tell me with whom you associate and I will tell you who you are. Nobility obliges. A used handkerchief should never be folded, or else. . . ."

It was an empty, eventless period, lacking in political and public action. People lived and died in the narrow ambience of the familiar. Time had established a single season in the city; it didn't seem to change, tied up in an impossible knot. The days were marked by two events that are the beginning and the end of every story: birth and death. People nourished themselves on the outdated events from the other side of the ocean. The umbilical cord linking them was already rotten, and the little that reached them through it was hot air, adulterated and lifeless: they fed themselves on fables.

When a little girl was born on the other side of the ocean, they celebrated her birth when she was walking all by herself and was starting to get into mischief, climbing up the branches of her family tree, looking for the green fruit of its hemophilia. If a king died on the other side of the world, they held his funeral when the royal body was already dust and the next-to-last generation of the worms that had eaten it had died.

When they canonized Saint Raimundo de Peñafort, they celebrated his rise to heaven when, on the other side, the saint hardly had any devotees left. But in any case, when the news came, preceded by bell ringing and fireworks, people rushed into the streets for the fiesta. The news shook off the morass, the *soroche* stood discreetly aside, and thus began the celebrations, which in general consisted of long Masses beginning at dawn with the setting off of a half-dozen Roman candles to chase away the demons and ended with religious processions and the running of the bulls, attended by all of the city's residents along with their families and their cortege of servants.

During one of the bull runnings María Illacatu's oldest son died in the most violent and ridiculous way possible, and ever since then, the Villacatus, Catovils, and Villa-Catós stopped attending the event, and not one member of the family has ever dared to break the tradition.

The day of the running of the bulls people congregated in the square from early in the morning and waited and waited for the most important guests to arrive so the fiesta could begin, and in turn the important guests—who included Señor Villacatu with seven of his fourteen children—each waited to be the last one to arrive, to give the impression that without him, and only him, not the bulls or the bullfighters, the fiesta couldn't start. Finally they all tacitly agreed to arrive together. The amorphous mass was acquiring monstrous proportions, with an enormous head with a thousand eyes and a thousand mouths that had begun to whistle impatiently and which almost changed the direction of the wind that brought the gusts of *soroche*.

Villa-Cató had mentally set his eyes on and seated himself in the place of honor. But one of the other important guests had done exactly the same thing, and as neither of the two wanted to yield because it would mean a loss of rank, prestige, and aristocracy, words became deeds, and before the very eyes of the spectators at the fiesta—who naively thought that the important guests' actions were a new addition to the fiesta, because from a distance that was what it looked like—the important guests, followed by their seconds and secretaries, went down to the sand and fought a duel, right in the center of the square.

The two bulls with frock coats and walking sticks measured their steps and saluted, and in the next instant both fired their pistols: Bruna's great-great-grandfather fell dead, owing more to good aim than to destiny, and the other man lost an ear.

What very few people knew about was the first and last dialogue the two duelers had at the end:

"Sir! I was here first!"

"I'm sorry, this is my place!"

"I'm telling you that I am not going to yield. . . ."

"If you think that I'm going to do it, you are wrong. . . ."(Pause.)

"Villain! I'm waiting!"

"Lowborn! Get out of my place!"

"Nobody calls me lowborn! I shall wash this affront away with your blood!"

"Here is my card!"

"Forget your card! We'll fight a duel!"

"I am the injured party!"

"But I am not descended from Indians!"

When the shots rang out, the echo flew out and brought Death back with it. Death came in a hurry and entered one of the victim's ventricles. Death came out of the mouth, dragging the soul with it in a crude bundle, rudely shoving aside the dead man's teeth and tongue that blocked its path. Then Death grabbed the echo by the throat and threw it far away, where it shattered on the mountaintops.

"A thunderclap, a thunderclap! It's God's punishment! . . ." people said.

Death hadn't planned on taking the other man's ear but did it in passing, without really wanting to. In sum: Bruna's great-great-grandfather went to the other world with the swiftness of a lightning bolt, without leaving a will, and the other man was left without an ear and with his honor.

One killed and one died for the sake of a meaningless vision, not knowing who the other man really was because he was wearing armor that was too brittle: his name.

The vanity of the city people and of Bruna's ancestors went on for years and years, incubating grudges, envy, crimes committed with impunity, and violence done to the most noble sentiments, which nobody protested. The superstitious cult of so-called nobility smothered them. It was a collective self-hypnosis needed to confront the world of public opinion, because in some cases the Indian blood was still evident; many people were still alive who remembered an Indian sitting in the garden beside the cursed well, her feet bare and her hair unbraided. Those who remembered the origins of the family names and fortunes were still alive.

This was what Bruna inherited: a world of inverted values in which blood had no function other than to indicate skin color, and tears were nothing but salt water. Dignity and common sense were cast in stereotyped roles. It was difficult to become a complete human being, a *sapiens sapiens,* shaking off one prejudice after another that adhered to her bones like flesh. It was painful to have been born in the city and to go out into the world and see that things had different values and weren't the way she had been taught,

or had learned, and then to have to start walking all over again—
and alone—in the opposite direction when she thought she had
almost arrived. . . .

Bruna was a product of fables, of legends, of time frozen like a
puddle of dirty water, of sadness, of the seasons, of the mountains,
but she kept searching for herself, until she found herself. . . .

6

After the tragic running of the bulls the widow retired to her house, accompanied by her solitude and the admiration of all.

"He was stretched out on the sand. . . ."

"That's how a noble dies."

"The poor widow with fourteen children!"

"Well, at least, with money . . ."

"Alone, but with honor . . ."

The widow couldn't adjust to her new state. Nothing consoled her or freed her from her sadness; her relatives and her fourteen children couldn't get her out of her rut. She was dying to know what her husband was doing in the great beyond. . . . She tried every method of communicating with the dead man. She chased his shadow through the dark rooms, where she burned fragrant herbs to counteract the smell of charred dove intestines, of lizard tails and popped-out frogs' eyes. She gazed in vain at the desolate nothingness of the crystal balls that she rubbed daily with her fingertips. She shuffled decks of cards in which jacks and aces trotted along mounted on suppositions. She patiently awaited the arrival of night, accompanied by her sobs and lamentations, but the dead man refused to appear. The widow didn't understand that he didn't want to come back and attributed her failures to the constellations not being in conjunction, or that, before sacrificing the doves, she hadn't washed her hands with the correct soap, or that the lizards, which played an important role in making spirits appear, weren't quite the proper shade of green, or that the herbs had been uprooted with the right hand instead of the left hand. So she searched, as they say, "from here to Mecca," saying quietly:

"I command you to come from beyond and listen to me. By these three crossed candles and this dove's blood, from my mournful blackness and in the name of the Father, the Son, and the . . ."

Widows didn't have any alternative but to docilely follow their husbands in death, the same as they had done in life. Women had no education whatsoever; they weren't even permitted to leaf through a book out of fear that they would become mannish. They were allowed contact only with the needle, the broom, and the cooking pots. When their thoughts dared to go beyond the eaves of their tile roofs, it was cause for scandal, and the women reprimanded themselves, because they believed that they were behaving badly. It was impossible for them to make any movements that hadn't been made before by their mothers and their grandmothers. The women were giant ovaries, dressed in black, where children were conceived one by one and with superstitions by the ton.

That was what the widow was like, believing in all of the era's superstitions. She never left the tablecloths spread out on the table after mealtime because she firmly believed that it would make the angels up in heaven start to cry. . . . She watched like a hawk, waiting for the moment when the last of her children finished eating to give the order to remove the tablecloths.

She believed that it was dangerous to go out into the street after a rainstorm wearing the color red, because the rainbow—which always chased after women—could make them mothers of albino children. The proof was that in the countryside there was a large quantity of albinos.

"No, he not mine! Don' you see he white? . . ."

"Mus' be child of mountain."

She believed that nobody should take a bath on Good Friday because doing so could make one turn into a fish, and she cited cases with the first and last names of the city residents who were sealed in fishbowls, whose families kept them alive by giving them breadcrumbs, hidden under the beds until they died, without a doubt, from drowning, and that they couldn't be killed or eaten, because being a murderer or a cannibal was strictly forbidden.

"In the Ayoras' house there's a closed, dark room that no one's allowed to enter."

"Why?"

"Because the youngest son is in there, under a bed, changed into a fish, for having bathed on Good Friday."

"You've seen him?"

"Yes. With these eyes that will one day be dust and ashes."

She wouldn't tolerate thirteen people sitting around the table because that surely meant one of the diners would die. Years later Bruna was dragged half-asleep from her bed and made to sit at the table with thirteen decrepit old people who were celebrating the diamond wedding anniversary of two of her relatives.

"For God's sake, the girl is asleep and she's going to fall out of her chair!"

"Asleep or awake, there are fourteen of us and not thirteen."

She believed that if a little bit of salt were spilled, out of carelessness, it brought the house bad luck, but that could be dispelled by tossing the rest of the salt over the left shoulder.

She believed that a black butterfly meant death and a white butterfly riches.

She believed that eating an avocado with sugar—which nobody ever did because it tasted terrible—was a mortal sin, but she couldn't explain why, or which commandment it broke.

"Never, never eat it, it's a sin."

"Why?"

"Because it is."

Laughter had to be controlled, because there would certainly be crying the next day if one had passed a certain limit. You had to swallow your happiness and think immediately of sad things.

"We can't, we can't laugh anymore. . . ."

"Yes. Tomorrow we'll cry all day. . . ."

When the twelve strokes of midnight struck on December 31, you could clearly see the future by dropping an egg white in a glass of water. When the Villacatus came back she did it and saw a white veil at the bottom of the glass, and she immediately began to prepare her bridal trousseau.

When the calendar said Tuesday the thirteenth, she made her fourteen children stay in bed. The doors weren't opened, or the windows, and a deathly silence reigned until the day was over.

Sometimes the house's inhabitants got out of bed and filed out, at twelve midnight, to urinate on a nettle bush so that any possible witchcraft—which some enemy of the family could have done to them—would be ineffective.

Every act of life was ruled by good and bad fortune. It seemed that the dead had nothing else to do but pass their lives playing dice or other games of chance on the skins of the living. Everything revolved around such nonsense. The widow was the high priestess of folly.

> Masses, pilgrimages, sacraments,
> divinations, witchcraft, enchantments . . .

Finally, when she felt that life was leaving her, owing to an unstoppable bleeding, she wrote in her own hand, and with her own blood, the names of Adam and Eve on two tiny pieces of tissue paper and applied them to her forehead, and she stayed that way for several days, waiting for the bleeding to stop. . . . But the blood was a string of thread that kept unraveling because Death had started to weave a red bonnet out of it. Nothing and nobody could make her change her mind; the widow remained firm in her beliefs until the final moment.

"Let the doctor come look at you. . . ."

"No, no, and no! The little papers are infallible! Besides, man's days are numbered. . . ."

One day she woke up with the feeling that her end was near,

because she had seen a black butterfly with its wings spread out and on them the shape of a skull and crossbones, just like a pirate's flag. From that moment on her only thought was of settling her accounts, without taking her eyes off the butterfly, which stayed attached to her bed curtain, like a sailboat waiting for good weather to set to sea, taking her soul with it on the long, long crossing. So she gathered her strength, rose out of bed, opened the windows that had been kept closed since her husband's death, and, full of determination, went out to put herself in contact with the night.

It was almost sunrise, a frigid, icy summer sunrise. The widow caught pneumonia. Staggering, anxious, lost in a world of omens and conjectures, consumed by fever, and with her eyes fixed on the black butterfly, she heard the crowing of the roosters and the sighs of the paving stones. When she bumped into the pneumonia, which arrived with a shiver, she heard it laugh when it read the bits of paper that were still glued to her forehead. Since the papers were backward, the pneumonia read the words as "mono" and "mona" and, dying of laughter, sat astride the widow's right lung. The terrified woman touched her side, sensing that a cold and unknown being had penetrated her, but she remained calm and searched the sky eagerly for what she had always been searching for; she knew that this was the moment to find it.

"The shooting star, the shooting star! . . . I have to see it. . . . My last opportunity. . . . Where, where is it, why can't I see it?"

The stars were out. The night looked down from above with hundreds of twinkling eyes. Everything was asleep, or pretending to be asleep. The imps lying on the tile eaves, their enormous hats pulled down over their ears, watched everything the city dwellers did, and they didn't miss the spectacle of the agonized widow. . . .

She kept looking for the shooting star that would fall from heaven and whose fall would take precisely the same amount of time as it would take her to say the Lord's Prayer. She sensed Death's presence the same way one senses all things that have already entered one's sphere of life, the same way that animals can sense the coming of rain or springtime without a calendar. Death was inside her, waiting for the shooting star and nothing else.

The family was awakened by the unusual noise of a window being opened so late at night, and also by a feeling that preceded the noise. They came running, barefoot, in their nightshirts, to the widow's room and knelt to watch the spectacle: the widow was gambling with the saving of her own soul. The fourteen children remained silent; even the smallest ones didn't dare let out a peep. After many hours, when the night had stopped being night, and many of those present had fallen asleep, they saw a shooting star fall from the sky, pulled, without a doubt, by the strings of despair. They recited the Lord's Prayer in the exact amount of time required and breathed easily: her soul was saved!

". . . butdeliverusofourdeathamen!"

"We made it, we made it! She was saved!"

"*Viva!* She was saved! *Viva!*"

"With her last words, but she was saved!"

It seemed like a party. A holy tranquillity invaded her when they put her in the bed. The *payachucho* had disappeared from the curtain. They brought the kids back to bed, gave them hot chocolate, covered them up, and told them that their grandma had been saved. The children slept peacefully. . . .

There was only one note of sadness in the house: the water from the fountain that cried ceaselessly and inconsolably. When day began to brighten, the widow was herself no more. Her arms were folded across her chest like a statue of a saint lying in state. The same blood-colored sheets became her shroud; it was her will.

Nobody could remove the bits of paper with the names of Adam and Eve on them from her forehead, and when they lifted her eyelids to look at her eyes, they were astounded to see that her pupils had disappeared and in their place was a shooting star, brilliant and fleeting.

They buried her with great solemnity. She was a privileged

human being. No one else in the city had managed to pull off the feat of the shooting star and the Lord's Prayer with such precision. She had gone straight to heaven from the place where one lived, died, and forgot, lost among the shadows of incantations, trapped in the viselike grip of portents and prophecies, spurred on by omens and guesswork.

Bruna liked to pass the hours sitting in the big chair where the widow had waited out nine months, fourteen times, while her children leavened inside of her. The widow's chair was the oldest piece of furniture in the house; the straw stuffing was poking through on all sides, but it was comfortable and invited you to throw yourself into the widow's rigidly patterned world and view it with much compassion: she had needed to believe in an existence that was governed by incomprehensible forces.

"Get out of the widow's chair, you'll catch her craziness. . . ."

"I don't want to! I'm playing:

> "*Vamos a Pifo*
> *a ver a mi hijo,*
> *que de puro viejo*
> *se ha hecho conejo.*
>
> "Let's go to Pifo
> to see my son,
> so old that out of habit
> he turned into a rabbit."

Confronted with the insecurity of the reeling world of the psyche, she had to search for a stronger and more durable grasp on this occultism. Otherwise nobody would be able to explain all the codes that had been imposed and accepted, all the rigid precepts that were obeyed, all the diffuse laws that kept people convinced right up to the moment of death, all the fiendish penalties that were venerated, and especially the all-powerful magic of *soroche*, which surrounded them at all times.

7

The children in Bruna's family were condemned to being orphans. Almost all of the children were raised and became adults absorbing their family's defects through osmosis. All of the widow's fourteen children, with the exception of the oldest one and another named Teresa, went to heaven without pain or glory. They died in infancy, victims of smallpox, whooping cough, and measles. The fourteen children lived under the tutelage of their aunts and uncles, who tried honorably to play the part of their parents but failed. The survivors used to sing at the top of their voices:

> Clara, Alfonsito, Cecilia, and Manuel: smallpox.
> Domingo, Margarita, Diego, and Raquel: measles.
> Petra, Ricardo, Eloisa, and Georgina: whooping cough.
> Teresita will soon be sick in bed
> and Carmela will soon be ready to wed. . . .

The aunts and uncles used up all of their energy in the marriage of the oldest daughter, Carmela, whom they married to a nobleman from the other side of the ocean, leaving the rest of the children to the mercy of nursemaids, and of sicknesses, and of their own destinies, which in any case were already fixed from the moment they were born, as it was already known that they would soon die. . . . The city's *soroche* went arm in arm with its fatalism.

"Margarita has a fever."

"She'll die soon. . . ."

"But—it's only a fever!"

"It doesn't matter, she won't make it past her second birthday."

The oldest daughter, Carmelia Catovil, passed into the family history with the name of Carmela the Tearful. They married her off when she was fifteen years old. It was a proxy marriage, arranged after the coming and going of copious correspondence on the backs of mules and the ocean. Her husband had a noble title, and she had money. . . . The girl's opinion wasn't consulted because it was known beforehand that the best thing that could possibly happen to a woman was to unite her destiny and her body to that of a nobleman. The noble was quite advanced in age, and in consideration of his age and position, the possessor of the title so cherished by the family's social ambition didn't come after the bride; she had to make the long and dangerous voyage herself.

"Carmela, you're going to get married."

"Good. When?"

"Next year."

"With whom?"

"With a nobleman."

"What's he like?"

"We don't know. He's not from here."

"Then . . . where is he from?"

"From Spain. You have to go there. . . ."

"I don't want to go! I don't want to go! I don't want to go!"

The voyage was full of difficulties and hardships. Of the two hundred travelers who accompanied the bride, more than half of them died en route or deserted in the face of the dangers and the depressing slowness of the crossing, which had to be done at a tortoise's pace so that the little bride would survive.

When Bruna learned the details of what her grandmother had had to put up with, she got furious because she knew that the trip wasn't so slow for the girl's sake, or out of consideration for her condition as a woman, but because it was a matter of transporting a virgin over the mountains to the sea. . . .

Carmela left amid the cheers of the crowd, hugs and advice from her aunts and uncles, and her younger siblings' tears, crying because they were losing the possibility of having a mother and figured that they were never going to see her again. She also cried rivers. Mounted on a mule's back and carrying in her arms two rag dolls with porcelain faces, she left the city, followed by a long caravan that was carrying her fabulous bride's trousseau, food for the difficult crossing, weapons for defense against the highway robbers, and tools for opening a path through the jungle.

When the first mule crossed the city limits, the last one still hadn't moved from the big gate of the Catovils' house. It was a trip not toward a determined place, but rather toward an idea. It was a pilgrimage in pursuit of a conventionalism. She was going not in search of a man, but in search of a position in society.

"Come look at little Carmela, who's leaving to go get married. . . ."

"So many mules! So many people! So much baggage!"

"Lucky her!"

Carmela never thought of rebelling, because at the time she was incapable of self-determination. The ideas she had been born with were rigidly adhered to her sex, and it would take her a long time to understand that the conditions of inferiority into which she had been born by the fact of her being a woman were not, in fact, real.

At the end of three months of crossing impregnable mountains, where one's breath was frozen by the cold of the high plains, and the diabolical mountain passes, they reached the end of their trip. But that would never make up for the burdens suffered. She would always remember, like a bad dream, the frozen gusts of wind that cut into her face, tattooing her with frost. The inhospitable hamlets that they had to approach with caution out of fear that they would not be well received. The heavy work that the guides and the mule drivers had to do, felling enormous trees in order to improvise a bed in which the joyless bride could pass the night. The hanging bridges that shot out over terrible precipices in whose depths a howling death unfolded before them. The swamps where the mules got stuck and had to be hauled out or abandoned to their fate. The places where the rain had been falling ever since the world evolved out of nothingness. The phantom cities that appeared and disappeared in a confused eyeblink. The kingdoms of malaria where the body twisted and shivered. The days and nights traveling to the coast, bringing a virgin who was going to get married to a name. For the few who managed to finish the trip, it was a nightmare. Carmela's body was tanned, and her spirit had strengthened with a hitherto unknown force.

"We're there!"

"Finally! And the girl is intact!"

"How could she not be, since their whole life is riding on her!"

A sailboat was rocking in the sea, waiting for the bride. She boarded the ship with her wet nurse, her trousseau, and her omens. The wind blew during the whole voyage. The crossing was completed without any major mishaps. The soul of her grandmother, María Illacatu, which was still hanging from the edges of the stars, pushed the ship until it reached a remote part of the earth, where it was assumed that the bride's troubles would be over.

But a fatal destiny awaited her: it had been born in August, with the last waning quarter of the moon, and that day, out of carelessness, her mother had caressed some magnolias, flowers whose vapors changed the design of the heavenly bodies.

They day before she left, the groom had died, tired and sad from waiting for her, or possibly he died of old age.

"The Count Don Emiliano de la Reguera y Soria? Pfff! He's six feet under ground."

"What?"

"I said that he's dead."

"When?"

"Oh, half a year ago, more or less. . . ."

"God help us! What did he die of?"

"Well . . . of old age, I think."

"Of old age, that can't be! He was my husband. . . ."

The dead man's family received her as a widow. The proxy marriage, contracted a year before, gave her certain prerogatives. Dazzled by the baggage she brought with her and by the jewel box that the wet nurse carried with her everywhere, they made her take over her husband's debts. Listening to the strange and painful misadventures of the trip, they offered her the empty loving care of relatives by marriage.

When Carmela turned sixteen, the old wet nurse, who never left her side from the moment she had come into the world, died of nostalgia for the distant city and also of sorrow for the misfortunes that had befallen the girl. The girl was left alone in a totally unfamiliar world. It was like a second birth without a father or a mother, without a wet nurse, without hand-embroidered blouses and lullabies.

Once free of this tutelage, she dedicated herself to consuming her trousseau, which disappeared little by little thanks to the whims she had begun to experiment with. One morning, an ice cream in the luxurious living room; one afternoon, a cup of tea on the fashionable terrace; then, a long mother-of-pearl cigarette holder; later, a trip to a city that all the pilgrims in the world visited; after that, some clothes because those she had brought with her were too small and also totally ridiculous. So, she happily continued to use up the contents of the jewel box.

She was a free woman, without prejudices. She was surrounded by the prestige of having come from such a faraway place and the mystery of being an almost married woman. Carmela de Villa-Cató opened herself up to life, obeying the impulses of her heart, which beat with an accelerated rhythm; fortified by pain, solitude, and adversities, she waited for the opportunity to conquer the world.

Outside the circle of her relatives by marriage, who were a continuation of the inhabitants of the city she had come from, she found people who were different from those who had been surrounding her. Her relatives by marriage resembled them, although without the weakness produced by *soroche*. When she realized that the world was populated by a different class of beings, she made the great discovery that the education she had been given was absurd: women could live at the margin of their "ghetto" and had unsuspected possibilities that could be explored without any catastrophe occurring.

She dedicated herself to traveling to wherever she wished, visiting astounding countries and places, but what helped her the most was contact with people. Her young virginal mind soaked up an extraordinary amount of culture. She learned various languages. She became a whole, absolute woman, mistress of her decisions and acts. She started to run her life in accordance with the impulses of her blood; she was the first and only woman at that time to cry out for a declaration of independence in the sleeping city.

Nevertheless, she couldn't free herself from the aura of being a femme fatale that she felt she had been marked with from birth, so little by little she developed a romanticism bordering on the vulgar from which she could never free herself, until a sickly sensibility began driving her actions and became the cause of her misfortune. Her era coincided with the dawn of a romantic period that produced the quintessence of fatal womanhood. And among other things, it seemed to her an incredible insult that they had baptized her with the name Carmela; and without consulting anybody, because it was nobody's business, she adopted the name Camelia: the flower that had a special quality among the heroines of her favorite novels. And with the name Camelia, the little money she had left, and much audacity, she threw herself into the world using the trampoline of her troubled years.

8

One boring day, when the autumn sun found her stretched out in bed and she thought she felt signs of *soroche* around her temples, she began to think that almost all women were like her, or could become like her, if they put their minds to it. On the other hand, in the distant city she would be the only example of this type. Because of her character and her aspirations, stretched out on the bed, the word "competition" was the omega of her alphabet; she shivered thinking about this and without further delay prepared for her return.

The roads hadn't changed much, but it was no longer a matter of the delicate bride who had to make the trip on a turtle's back, but of a woman who could physically compete with the robust mule drivers and psychologically stop a band of criminals in their tracks with the strength of her tongue. Her return trip lasted as long as one of the lamentations of the first trip. When she arrived in the city of her childhood, she saw that nothing had changed, except that the children had grown up or died, and of all her brothers and sisters only one remained.

Her plans worked out as she imagined. As soon as she arrived, the city started stirring.

"Carmela's back!"

"Which Carmela?"

"Catovil, the one who left a few years back to get married. . . ."

"The one who neither did nor didn't?"

"Yes, her!"

Camelia was a flesh-and-blood piece of news. Everyone wanted to see her and hear, from her brightly painted red lips, the adventures she had lived through.

The Catovils' house was once again filled with noises and hurried steps to welcome the newly arrived woman, whom they had given up for dead. The imps of the house put on new clothes. The weeds were pulled out of the garden at once. The windows of the front rooms were opened. The furniture was polished. Dust that had accumulated for years was wiped away. The railings and the doors leading to the corridors were given their second coat of paint, in the same shade of bright green. The moss that was covering the stones of the fountain was scraped off.

Camelia became the city's center of attraction, especially for the men, for whom the house of Bello-Animal—the only spicy place tolerated in the city—sporadically stopped existing. The women of the Bello-Animal lamented:

"Things have been very bad ever since she arrived. . . ."

"Let's move the piano out onto the balcony. . . ."

"We're going broke! The pricks are cheating us!"

"We've got to do something! We're going down for the third time!"

The men started consuming large quantities of pills to combat the ills of *soroche*. Camelia kept them all excited with the splendor of her plunging necklines, which she wore at all hours of the day without seeming to notice the acute cold that blew down from the mountains. To the men, it seemed like a feat of heroic and warlike proportions, that a woman could be a widow, single, and married all at the same time, and they were amazed that she had been able to travel alone without dying and to subsist without a lady escort accompanying her to these strange and faraway places. They couldn't sleep at night thinking about it and trying to figure out if Camelia was still a virgin, and they would have given anything to find out with whom, where, and how that which maybe hadn't happened could have happened. . . .

"She's been halfway around the world. . . ."

"Yes, you know . . . all by herself. . . ."

"Is she . . . ? Would she be . . . ? Well, you understand my meaning."

"I understand, oh yes, I understand. . . . It's a very delicate matter."

She knew what she was doing to the men of the city, who could proudly say:

"Last night I spent a delicious evening at the Villacatós' house. . . ."

Which certainly sounded different from saying:

"Last night I spent a delicious evening at the house of the Bello-Animals."

She exploited the situation she was presented with to the maximum and with true talent. The possessor of certain attractions and of a school of coquetry never before seen, she felt herself to be at the pinnacle of her existence, while her family cursed the moment that it occurred to her to come back to the city in order to put such an honorable name on display. . . .

"For God's sake, Carmela, don't do that!"

"Camelia, Aunt, please, Ca-me-lia!"

She had the gift of offering herself without giving herself. The men were perplexed, not knowing what to do. They were accustomed to the obscene temptations of the Bello-Animal. Camelia, on the other hand, said yes and then later negated that with an innocent no full of roundabout intellectual double-talk that only increased their masculine lust for her.

"Camelia, divine Camelia, may I . . ."

"What, Don Julian? Tell me, tell me!"

"Well . . . well . . . address you in the familiar form? . . ."

"Oh, is that all?"

She could attract and then repel, always keeping distance between the bodies, when wills and intentions had already tacitly united, which produced sensations in the men similar to that of sitting on hot coals.

The only time the women of the city ever joined together in a bloc in the name of their common defense was when they united in solidarity against Camelia, siding with the women of the Bello-Animal, whom they stopped calling "loose women" in favor of "those poor women."

Those poor women hadn't been economically affected. On the contrary, the customers who came by were the same dirty old men who visited Camelia's house, but their visits were quick, to the point.

"Don Nicanor! You don't send us flowers anymore. . . ."

"Well, you see . . ."

"Oh, of course, we understand. . . . The flowers are for her. . . ."

The united bloc for common defense included the mothers of all the marriageable daughters and all the possible future mothers in the city. It included nuns from the convents and servant maids from the rich people's houses. Impelled by the circumstances, the women dedicated themselves to spreading all manner of gossip and lies. Minds shook off their lethargy and allied themselves with tongues, and when the tongues refused to say certain things, then they allied with the hands.

"Have you heard the latest?"

"About that . . . ?"

"Yes, they say she's . . ."

"And which of our husbands is . . . ?"

"Who knows? With so many men going in and out . . . of that house."

They wrote a story that could be read from a distance, written with broad strokes, of offended honors, wrecked homes, of cozy, sleep-filled nights, of infidelities, of cruelties, and of all the things that common and ordinary women say when they get together to talk about their husbands. All of this was written on the facade of the Villacatós' house. This story was repeated and repeated every time two women got together; they talked in low voices with their heads together, making certain signs with their hands, shaking their heads and blushing.

Camelia was guilty of nothing more than being a woman of the world. They couldn't pardon the grace and wit with which she handled the masculine sex of the city, or her cultivation, or her self-fulfillment, or even her wardrobe, which looked deliciously extravagant. Or the large doses of perfume with which she enveloped her figure, leaving a wake of unknown fragrances and unsatisfied desires. Or the furs and silks. Or the enormous mother-of-pearl box in which she lined up Egyptian cigars. She was the only woman in the city who had ever been seen smoking; not even the women of the Bello-Animal had been granted this license. Her other great sin was ignoring the rest of the women.

"Carmela, you're going to be ruined! Everyone's talking about you. . . ."

"Who is everyone?"

"All the women."

"I don't care! Better!"

She acted as if she always had a cortege of fanatical admirers at her feet. She was actually rather ugly, but tall, elegant, and very thin, just as someone who made a great show of congenital romanticism should have been. She used two or three false birthmarks that she made herself by cutting up a piece of black velvet and putting glue on the back. She was the one who introduced the fashion of velvet. People who weren't used to the word—the *v* and the *b* sounding the same—called it "bellbet." She had abundant, very black hair. During the day she wore it pulled back with a tortoiseshell clasp set with jewels, and at night she let it fall loosely around her shoulders to give the impression of her long, lanky figure being a nocturnal apparition. Her evening clothes were cut in the Greek style, which was the cause of another scandal, since the rest of the women used only one set of clothes for the home and another to go out into the street, not for select hours of the day. Camelia the Tearful's clothes exposed her emaciated arms, but as thin as they were, the men of the city dreamed of being held prisoner in them.

"I don't know what the men see in her, with her bones sticking out and those black seeds on her face. . . ."

"With her black hair like an Indian's and her face as pale as if she had tuberculosis. . . ."

She breakfasted on the juice of several limes in order to accentuate the pallor of her face, and she painted large violet-colored rings around her eyes, so that everyone would know about her constant insomnia produced by the pangs of love. At five in the afternoon she put on a silk kimono and drank her tea in authentic red porcelain teacups. She did four hundred bends in front of the mirror to maintain her waspish waist, since she wanted a strong hand to be able to encircle it.

She was skilled in the art of fainting when the circumstances demanded it; and when she did it, she did it with an artist's conviction.

"The salts, the salts! Our Camelia has fainted!"

"It's all your fault, Don Martín, you know how that passage from the divine Mr. Hugo affects her. . . ."

Following the fashion that she had seen in several cities on the other side of the ocean, every Tuesday night she gathered in her salons the most distinguished of the literati, who were mostly poets, and the occasional painter who had been transported to the profitable threshold of fame. She brought the nine muses down from Olympus to sit on her guests' knees, so that nothing should be lacking and that they should all feel more at home at her gatherings.

The sculptors, who, with the passage of time, were to become the most noteworthy artists of the city, were never invited to Camelia the Tearful's soirées. They were considered to be mere artisans. People figured that the way they cut up tree wood made them ordinary woodcutters. When they brushed off the blocks and their feet were surrounded by wood shavings, they slipped among the glory, clouds, archangels, and saints who lay sleeping in their disorderly studios. And when they rubbed with sheep bladders to give that special shine to the marble statues, their hands lost the finesse of the writers' hands and the characteristic style of gentlemanly visitors holding a glass of Baccarat crystal between their fingers.

Nor were there theater people. There was no interest in the stage, perhaps because they all acted twenty-four hours a day. Theater companies that toured the world never reached the city; the roads that led to it still dropped off suddenly into canyons through which they could travel only with the scenery on their backs, fear in their masks, pantomime in their eyes, wearing buskins that stuck like cupping glasses to the earth so as not to slide in the mud, waiting for the sun's footlights to light up and frighten off the damned amateur actors who were keeping the professional actors from making their entrance in the city that had never raised its curtain to the world.

Camelia the Tearful was the only woman at her gatherings. They talked of art and literature. Camelia recited poetry in the sweetest French. She tried out long paragraphs from *The Sorrows of Young Werther* that she knew by heart. The guests never tired of hearing her, with their hands folded and their eyes closed, trying to apprehend the words, the silences, and the intentions. When she finished, the old family house shook with clamorous applause that woke up the ghosts. A faint dust fell from the walls, and all present felt as in their element as if they were drowning in a sea of ink, with little paper ships and oars made out of swans' feathers, where the fish were letters and the sea an immense ocean of poetry.

Camelia the Tearful's hegemony even reached the point of figuring in the oracle of politics: she kept up a copious correspondence with all the insurrectionist and expatriated exiles; she amused herself by inflaming and squelching barrack uprisings and rebellions, according to her mood. They conspired on a grand scale at her literary gatherings, they overthrew governments and forged revolutions as if it were a way of passing the dull hours.

"The revolution will break out tomorrow!"

"Yes, Camelia can't resist General Arévalo's mustache any longer. . . ."

She got the name Camelia the Tearful from her long, thick eyelashes, darkened with ointments made from the marrow of human bones and the wicks of tallow candles—which was the current lighting supply for the city's poor people. The ointments were sold at the entrances to the cemeteries under the name of "life-giving ointments." On the evenings of her gatherings, Camelia succeeded in placing on the tip of her lashes, with true mastery, a drop of clear oil to produce the impression of a tear hanging from the tip of her feminine sensibility. While bearing this tear, Camelia the Tearful got everything she wanted. Men couldn't resist the twinkling of the perennial tear and did whatever she asked them to do, especially with her hair all disheveled and a companion tear soon joining the first.

"General Arévalo has to be replaced by Colonel Torres."

"Camelia! That's madness!"

"No it isn't, Torres is more romantic, he reminds me of Napoleon!"

"But, Camelia . . ."

"I think I'm going to cry. . . ."

Torres took over, and Camelia the Tearful's gatherings returned to their literary shade. Fine liqueurs were served, brought from the other side of the ocean on the mules' raw backs. Camelia the Tearful served the wine with infinite grace, and when she spoke the ritual words "To your health," everyone automatically drank two-thirds of their glasses; then they said, "To your health," and finished them off.

At nine o'clock homemade hot chocolate was served that had been distilled and hand ground in a hollow stone. Once the hot chocolate was consumed, it took effect, and from the most passionate political discussion, or languid literary dissertation, they passed to the topic of love.

Impelled by the circumstances, by never-satisfied desires, as if by the fire that was ignited by Camelia the Tearful's presence and figure, all of the guests at her parties had declared their love for her. They had exhausted the topic in all of its shades, variations, results, and consequences, not in fact, but on the platonic plane.

The Tuesday nights went on for year after year. The guests had a few more gray hairs, a longer mustache, a larger bald spot, a slightly bigger belly, and they brought with them some sonnets or a bouquet of flowers for the mistress of the house.

9

The years went by with their habitual slowness in the sleeping city, and when Camelia the Tearful's unshakable fortitude started to crumble because there wasn't a single man left who hadn't declared his most fervent adoration for her, through oral or written means, in prose or in verse, she granted her hand to the person whom she was least expected to choose. She acted on a whim, obeying the senselessness of the days when her body was ruled by the vacillating logic of the moon. The first signs of *soroche* were becoming visible. She was wearing a cement blindfold around her eyes. Camelia the Tearful resolved to accept one of her suitors when she was well into her forties, which even though she didn't look it, she was. She realized that the game she had gotten used to playing couldn't be kept up indefinitely, since the infusions of rosemary water no longer made her first gray hairs disappear completely.

The chosen one was in her judgment a luminary. He was ten years older than she was and swore by all the muses that he had remained single waiting for a passionate and tempestuous love, as only Camelia the Tearful could offer him. The truth was quite different. . . .

"Camelia, I've been waiting fifty years, my whole life, for you!"

"Then you won't have to wait anymore."

"Oh, what happiness! I swear that I have never even laid eyes on another woman!"

"You liar!"

"Camelia, my heart, you have been the only one! Bowing at your feet, I beg to receive the white marble of your hand."

The wedding was very elegant, the smallest details supervised by the refined and romantic spirit of she who had decided to cross the bridge that she had been trying to cross since she was fifteen years old. Camelia the Tearful wanted to have twenty boys dressed—or rather undressed—as Cupid accompanying the cortege. But the sleeping city's inhabitants raised a cry to heaven, and Camelia had to go along with twenty girls dressed in pink with crowns made of orange blossoms on their heads.

For the third time they painted the railings in that same shade of bright green as always. They varnished the furniture. Once again they cleaned the cobwebs from the corners and weeded the garden. The little mermaid on top of the fountain was polished with lime peels and bicarbonate. The vertebras in the entranceway were cleaned with hot water and ashes. French champagne was ordered and arrived the moment the bride was leaving the church. They erased the denigrating story that had been written on the house's facade. The women of the sleeping city breathed easily, after living so long on tenterhooks, and prepared to attend the wedding. The rejected suitors started frequenting the house of the Bello-Animal again: the single men openly; the married men surreptitiously. Those who were poets spitefully vulgarized the words "wedding bed," and there were two or three attempts at suicide. . . .

Camelia the Tearful, dressed in white—which in reality was accurate in spite of the fact that she was both married and a widow—left people staring openmouthed as she left the church arm in arm with her chosen one. She looked young and slender, without the thick violet rings of insomnia around her eyes, and the tears that she used to make each eye bear had disappeared, since they had no reason to exist anymore.

The residents of the sleeping city talked about Camelia the Tearful's wedding for a long time, pondering her gown and the banquet that they had that day. Everyone was waiting for the great event to culminate with the arrival of an offspring who would inherit the father's supposed talent and the mother's money and imponderable graces.

But the event never arrived. The father, refined artist that he was, said he had to create the proper atmosphere in order to enter into the preliminary functions of exercising his paternity. . . .

During his long half century of life, he had never met a woman who was able to create an atmosphere like Camelia the Tearful. She could do the impossible; she could even make a stone break out in a sweat. A little bit concerned, he couldn't stop thinking about his rare and useless visits to the house of the Bello-Animal.

"Don Julián isn't the man for the Catovil woman."

"No. But they say he's taking Spanish-fly wings in syrup."

"Even if he ate them raw! With or without Spanish fly, he can't do it!"

"But with her he has to be able to. . . ."

Camelia the Tearful knew about life from the actions of the heroes in her favorite books. She hoped that her wedding night would be unique—which it certainly was. She didn't catch on when her supposedly fiery-spirited husband asked her to sing, once she was between the white linen sheets—embroidered with little Cupids by the diligent hands of the Conceptas nuns—the children's song *"Matan-tirun, tirun-lá."* Camelia the Tearful, between surprise and pleasure, spent the whole night singing, and the light of dawn took her by surprise, with her voice hoarse from singing:

> *Buenos días, su señoría,*
> *Matan-tirun, tirun-lá.*
> *¿Qué deseaba, su señoría?*
> *Matan-tirun, tirun-lá.*
> *Yo deseo una de sus hijas.*
> *Matan-tirun, tirun-lá.*
> *En qué oficio la pondría.*
> *Matan-tirun, tirun-lá . . .*

Good morning, Your Lordship,
Matan-tirun, tirun-lá.
What is your wish, Your Lordship?
Matan-tirun, tirun-lá.
I want one of your daughters.
Matan-tirun, tirun-lá.
What do you want to do with her?
Matan-tirun, tirun-lá . . .

Other nights went by, and Camelia the Tearful started to lose hope, suspecting her husband's somewhat underdeveloped world. It wasn't easy for her to give up all her illusions, and since she had a very generous nature, she opted for changing the lyrics of the children's song, making them red hot. Certain words and meanings were extremely obvious. It wasn't easy at first, and she blushed while singing, but she conquered her natural repugnance and went through with it to prove that she had done all she could.

The nights grew long, slow, and tedious, with her singing songs that she hadn't sung since she was a little girl and which, on top of all that, had no effect at all, in spite of the fact that Don Julián swore that it would be the last time she would have to sing. The days were sad, cloudy with shame and memories and sprinkled over with a thick layer of long silences.

The anxiously awaited child, the event that they had talked about from the time they shipped her off, never arrived. . . . Every day she grew thinner and more exhausted from singing "*Matan-tirun, tirun-lá.*" Her family, worried, hounded her with questions.

"Camelia! What's the matter with you? Every day you're paler and more deteriorated. . . ."

"It's not for nothing!"

"Tell us: you're not getting along with your husband!"

"Husband! Don't talk to me about him!"

Camelia the Tearful had lost the prestige of being the cock of the literary henhouse. The parties and gatherings lost their sheen. She started to feel a weariness and a lack of appetite for life that translated into a black feeling toward everything that surrounded her. She spent long hours sitting next to the fountain, watching the water flow, with a book open in her hands that she never read.

Until one day it struck her all of a sudden what a big lie everything was, and, after making a fire in the middle of the patio, she burned all the books that had been the delights of yesteryear, burned her dreams one by one, threw all her sumptuous clothing out of the closets, took off her jewels, abandoned her large mother-of-pearl cigarette holder, the piece of glue-covered "bellbet" that she made her false birthmarks with, the small Baccarat crystal glasses—those that later on Mama Chana would mistakenly call "cabaret" glasses—and, after silently caressing the fountain's little mermaid, who accompanied her in her pain and humiliation, she left the Catovils' house, slamming the door definitively behind her, in search of her lost hopes, mounted on the Rocinante of her disillusion and with two genuine tears in her eyes.

She was a female Quixote looking for a chimera, and as such, she headed for the only place in the sleeping city that she had looked upon with much distrust. She figured that nobody would come up with the idea of looking for her there, in the convent of the Conceptas nuns who had embroidered her wedding sheets.

When she got there, she pulled the little bell rope, made certain that no one had seen her, and when they opened the other side of the grating, and she said who she was and what she was there for, she gave a satisfied sigh and entered.

The convent celebrated with three days of merrymaking. The nuns received her like the lost sheep of the flock. They celebrated the return of the repentant sinner, and as all of the nuns had forgotten how to read and write, they made her their superior, but not before quickly cropping her hair and dressing her in the thick veils that turned day into evening and evening into night.

The useless and rejected husband searched for her in vain. Burdened with shame, he looked for her on all fours, under the beds and chairs, at the bottom of the linen chests, among the bits of soft, fine cloth that the widow used to make baby clothes, lifting the covers off the cooking pots, and he even ventured to look into the bottom of the well, but . . . in vain. One day he convinced himself that she had been ravished and carried off to another country by one of her lovers from the other side of the ocean. Then he cried for her as if she were dead. He diligently dressed in mourning for the rest of the years of his life, and he remained alone in the old house, writing passionate verses to Camelia's memory, to her marble white body, to her long, thin hands and her titillating tear, until he, too, felt bored of living and of writing nothing but words and more words and died—as the city folk said—of the purest and most passionate love.

"Don Julián just died. . . ."

"He died of love."

"Where could Camelia the Tearful be?"

"Who knows!"

Years went by, and Camelia the Tearful's memory still lived in the hearts of lovers of the arts and of other lovers who sometimes, very late at night, walked the outskirts the sleeping city, looking for her footprints. Children learned to jump rope while singing:

> *Monja, viuda, soltera, y casada . . .*
> *Monja, viuda, soltera, y casada. . .*
>
> Nun, widow, single, and married . . .
> Nun, widow, single, and married . . .

10

Camelia the Tearful's only remaining sister had just died after giving birth to her ninth child. It was the most natural and common of deaths, dying of postpartum fever. It seemed like a curse of the Illacatus that their descendants should all be orphans and that the children would all be brought up by their aunts and uncles.

The news reached Camelia the Tearful by accident through the revolving serving hatch to the outside world that one of the Conceptas sisters was operating. The news turned into sighs and cries from the nuns. Under the dead woman's pillow the family found a piece of paper in which she asked Camelia to take care of the nine orphans:

"Dear Carmela: My heart tells me that you are not dead and that you are also not abroad. . . . I beg you to look after my nine children. Be a mother to them. Remember that there were fourteen of us, too, and that only we survived, you . . . and I, who am dying. . . . Your sister, Teresa."

As the superior of the convent, Camelia the Tearful couldn't just abandon her nuns, so she asked for a papal dispensation from Rome. While waiting for it to arrive, she set herself to preparing the most qualified nun to succeed her. The most qualified one was seventy-three years old, and, like all the rest, she had forgotten how to read and write. So Camelia the Tearful immediately set to teaching her spelling all over again:

"*P* and *a* makes 'pa.' *P* and *e* makes 'pe.' *P* and *i* makes 'pi.' . . ."

While the dispensation documents came and went on the backs of mules and the crests of the waves, and the nun learned how to read and to write, many years went by and the nine orphans were reduced to three. When Camelia the Tearful finally had the dispensation in her hands, she left to take possession of the old mansion, site of her triumphs and failures, with a willful temperament that amazed and edified the Conceptas sisters, who said tearful good-byes to her, loading her down with medallions and little images of the saints for her nieces and nephews.

Nothing had changed in the sleeping city. The children had grown, and the old had died. The old house was filled with shadows, dust, and memories. The little mermaid was still perched on top of the fountain, holding the same conch as always in her hands. The two nieces and a nephew were standing in line to meet her, dressed in black, with their eyes wide open. The ghosts that she had ordered shut up in the back rooms of the house, when she was a woman of the world, were now running around loose through the hallways, knocking everything over. The garden had been taken over by weeds and nettles. The breath of a great many dead people remained stuck in the cracks in the plaster walls.

All those years in the convent had turned Camelia the Tearful into a different woman: she had torn the smile from her face. When she took her heart out to wash off the worldly sophistications to which she had dedicated herself before, she found she couldn't put it back in the same place, but instead positioned it near her kidneys. She had stopped being a cultured woman who shocked the men of the sleeping city, and the only thing she read during her years of being cloistered was *The Imitation of Christ* by Señor Kempis and the paper that her sister Teresa had sent her before she died.

She had been living in a world where the reality of things was known to be an illusion. She had left the best of herself behind between the convent walls, as well as her reputation as a saint and a sage. She was silent, austere, and cold. She still had her dominant character. She had commanded the nuns because of who she was, and she dominated her nieces and nephew with the strength of her gaze, reinforced and punctuated by her long eyelashes, which weren't thick anymore but were still imposing. The nieces and nephews didn't dare to breathe in her presence. Thank heaven the other six had already gone, victims, as always, of measles and small-pox. The three who remained were Catalina, Francisco, and Clarita.

The three of them grew up within the narrow circle of an education dominated by fear and uncertainty of the sudden changes they experienced—between the tedium of the long, convent-influenced prayers, the tyrannies of a woman who had stopped being human because of disillusion, and the grief and anxiety they felt seeing the wide hallways and not being able to run through them or play with the water from the fountain. . . .

When their aunt heard them singing the children's song "*Matan-tirun, tirun-lá,*" she lost her head and everyone had to run and hide in the garden. The children hid in the back of the closets or in the trunks, where perfumed letters tied with colored ribbons were still kept. The servants, trembling, brought her big cups of soothing *toronjil* and orange-blossom tea; they gave her one hundred drops of calming *serenita* water, and their aunt sank into the world of uncon-sciousness. Only then did the children take each other by the hand and go out to sail on the sea of tranquillity.

Camelia the Tearful's attacks were fearsome. She couldn't live in the house where she had stopped being who she was; life demand-ed too much of her. She still hadn't forgiven herself for having allowed herself to be fooled by an insignificant, miserable little man; and her destiny didn't stop there, since having experienced mascu-line inconsistency for herself, she contemptuously generalized all of its implications onto the stronger sex. Because of this she began to force her nephew, Francisco, to dress like a girl until the day he went to school. . . .

"I don't want anything masculine in this house."

"What do you mean, 'masculine'?"

"Men!"

"Aunt, what about the tomcat?"

"Have him taken far away and bring back a female cat."

The two nieces and the nephew who survived the death of their parents and their childhood sicknesses were the effigy of her failure. She never knew how to treat them; her acid heart had shriveled up, and she was incapable of showing any tenderness. With her, the last branch of María Illacatu's first son dried up forever.

11

Near the big family house, next to the budding cherry tree—the one that dropped its fruit all over the orchard and the neighboring patios—a fiery glow could be seen ever since they built the house. Every night a strange, cold, blue flame appeared out of the depths of the earth and disappeared just as quickly if someone came near the spot and tried to look directly at it. So the flame moved elsewhere: from the base of the tree it passed through the pupils of the eyes and lodged itself in the brain. Anyone who looked at the flame, and then closed their eyes, would still see it for hours before it faded beneath the greedy eyelids.

"Look at the blue flame! There it is again!"

"See how it shrinks and grows!

"That's where the treasure is!"

"Let's dig!"

"And what if the treasure isn't meant for us?"

They believed that the flame was the soul of a miser who had buried his treasure and that his soul had to stay behind, guarding it until it reached the hands of its rightful owner. . . .

María Illacatu's precious glass jewels and emeralds had disappeared sooner than expected. None of her three children thought of working: Work is for Indians, they said. The first son, the one who died at the bullfights, dedicated himself to parties and soirées, trying to cement and maintain a social rank that didn't yet have the desired opposite to go with his purchased title. . . . The second one entered a monastery, following the tradition of all second children. And the third one was Panchito, who put himself in dire economic straits trying to keep his large family living in the manner to which they had become accustomed. So he decided to claim the treasure and made meticulous preparations as indicated by the books of the time on how to find buried treasures:

"*Manual—Effectiveness Guaranteed—On the Art, Manner, and Form of Finding and Claiming Hidden Treasures.* Printed in the city of Lima, Peru, under Ecclesiastical License."

Pancho waited for the full moon to come. He had a three-month-old *llamingo* brought in that had been fed only on dry grass and *piquiyuyo* cactus flower. A black dog with two white spots: one on its back and the other in the shape of a half-moon on its forehead. He got hold of four sacred candles that were supposed to have burned in all-night vigil over the body of a young maiden. . . . A pitcher of hard cane liquor—the cane must have grown near a river where women bathed. . . . Brand-new picks and shovels that had to be blessed not by a priest but by a drunken sacristan. . . . The preparations dragged on for months, with attendant expectations.

The family never got rid of the pitcher of cane liquor. Bruna saw it with the old furniture that was stored in the back rooms of the house. It was full of cobwebs and had a greenish sediment at the bottom.

"What could be at the bottom of the pitcher?"

"I don't know, but don't ever touch it. . . ."

"Why not?"

"Because it could be poison, or still contain antimony from the treasure."

When the full moon was in the exact position indicated in the manual, Panchito gathered all of his family, friends, and buddies who were known throughout the city for using the most curses and went to the garden, bringing all the necessary tools. Clutching stalks of the miraculous San Cipriano plant, they took up positions around the cherry tree and watched as these natural wands pointed toward the place indicated by the flame. The stems were bending with such force that they had to be held with both hands.

"Help me, Manuel, the stems are pointing here!"

"This is the right place for sure!"

"Dig! Dig! Hurry!"

Long after midnight, when the ringing of the pickaxes drowned out the grumblings of souls in pain, when the sky over the lemon trees started to brighten as if the color were fading out of the night and the roosters were waking up with a fluttering of their wings but not crowing yet, they found a chest made of hard black leather. The men took big gulps of liquor, and their vocabulary became violent:

"Goddamn the—!"

"S.O.B. . . ! X . . . y . . . z . . . !"

"Well, c . . . my w . . . !"

The dog shook the half-moon from its forehead, and it fell and broke into pieces; the *llamingo* turned four months old; and the sacred candles were blown out. They dug out around the chest so they could tie ropes around it and hoist it up to the surface more easily. But Pancho couldn't resist the temptation of being the first one to open the trunk, and before it was all the way up, he jumped to the bottom of the pit and, using a piece of iron as a crowbar, forced the locks and opened the chest. Everyone there shouted with amazement when they saw that it was completely full with coins of the purest gold:

"Leave me! Leave me alone! C . . . m . . . t . . . !"

"Wait, Panchito, wait! M . . . $ñ$ . . . O . . . ! Don't be an a—!"

"Ayyy!"

The shouting was so loud that they woke up Panchito's wife, who had been prohibited from participating in the search for treasure because she was a woman (women impeded the success of the job). Panchito stroked the gold pieces, buried his arms in the chest, and was wallowing in them when his wife appeared. Then everyone saw something that made their hair stand on end: the strongbox suddenly closed, jumped out of the pit, and disappeared into the darkness of the night. . . . They had violated the first rule, third section, of the book on digging up treasure: the complete absence of any women, and there stood the aunt in her nightshirt, with her mouth wide open.

"*La señora! C* . . . *m* . . . *q* . . . !"

"Go! Leave! Get lost! Don't be a *c* . . . !"

"It's her fault the trunk's getting away!"

"We lost everything because of a *t* . . . *u* . . . *v* . . . !"

It was nearly daytime when everybody left with their heads down, looking stupefied. Panchito went to bed using all the curses that he had learned that night on his wife—who remained with her mouth wide open, understanding nothing of what had happened.

When she brought the cocoa to his bed around midday to wake him up, she found him dead. . . .

Family and friends rushed to see him: he was clutching a gold doubloon in his fist, and he looked as though he were sleeping, even laughing out of one side of his mouth. Nobody could remove the gold piece because his hand had closed around it forever, adhering it to his palm. . . .

The doctors said that antimony from the treasure had entered his lungs via the cartilage on the left side of his nose, which was as black as if it had been burned. The soul of the treasure had followed the beaten path of good and bad smells, had reached his heart, and paralyzed him. Anyway, he took the gold piece with him to his grave, which was shocking for people to see.

"They say that nobody could open his hand. . . ."

"The solid gold doubloon was stuck to his flesh!"

The death knell rang out in the sleeping city for two straight days. The next day his wife followed him docilely to the grave, perhaps afflicted with a guilt complex. The doctors didn't say that, but rather that her death was due to some strange disease, which they diagnosed as lockjaw. In any case, she died while turning all black and twisted like the roots of the old cherry tree that dropped its fruit all over the orchard and the neighboring patios.

"Panchito's widow is really bad. . . . She won't last the night!"

"All because of that treasure."

"Because the treasure wasn't meant for them. . . ."

They arranged the funerals. Another group of orphans wandered around the house again. Everyone had to wear black again. They removed the mirrors from the big rooms again. They hung black crepe around the edges of the portraits of their ancestors. Once again they closed the windows facing the street so that the small amount of noise from the sleeping city wouldn't disturb the house in mourning. For forty nights they prayed for the souls of the departed who had left the world of the living under such unusual circumstances. Night after night the family members repeated the story of the treasure chest, without leaving out a single detail, until they grew tired of it. When visitors reported it to others, and the story was reproduced down through the generations, it ended up saying that Uncle Panchito had buried the treasure at the foot of the old cherry tree, and when Bruna's generation came along, her brothers were always trying to hunt for Panchito's treasure.

"You want to go to the garden to dig for the treasure?"

"Let's go! Then we can curse all we want."

"No women allowed. . . ."

"Bruna can go if she wears my pants!"

Once again the house lived through a new period of muteness and silence, barely disturbed by the water coming out of the fish's mouth. The well with the eye of the Devil in it once again grew murky with self-importance. While living with their aunts and uncles, the nieces and nephews took on the attitudes of the elderly and began feeding themselves on the produce of hypocrisies and conventionalisms. Death settled into the house once and for all, and sadness gushed from everyone's eyes.

"The hermit was singing; who's going to die?"

"There's a black butterfly in the parlor; who has it come to take away?"

Midwives went in and coffins went out through the big door of the old house with an alarming frequency. Every corner of the house had a story about someone who had died under such and such circumstances. The ritual of death kept up a savage barbarity that took centuries to disappear. The difficulty of explaining the things from the great beyond, which seemed to be controlled by the cruelest beings, made death into a morbid event that would never go away. Whenever some family member died, Bruna cried, but she cried because she dreaded wrapping herself in black clothing; most of the time she couldn't have cared less about the deceased, but she had to dress in black for many months, and when she finally started to wear semimourning clothes, another one would die and so on indefinitely. . . .

"Put your colorful clothes away in the chest."

"You have to dress in black for eight months."

"Again?"

"Uncle Anselmo died."

"And who is Uncle Anselmo?"

12

Alvaro de Villa-Cató was one of Panchito's sons. Everyone called him Alvarito. He died at the chronological age of eighty-five, but he barely had the mental age of a four-year-old. He was an adult child-genius. He spent his whole life sitting at a loom, weaving a red carpet. All the days and hours of his life, he never did anything but weave the carpet that he could never finish, the carpet that the Holy Father would walk upon all the way from Rome to the sleeping city.

This dream fed his whole life. The red carpet was tightly woven and was as even, soft, and smooth as a woman's cheek. And as Alvarito's hands grew more skillful on the crude loom that he had installed in his own room, the weaving kept getting more and more perfect.

The carpet was rolled up on itself, and every day it got harder to turn, until it became so big that it pushed up through the roof and broke through the floor. It was one meter wide and as long as a lifetime, like an unimaginably huge red snake hibernating for the winter. It would reach around the world and float upon the waters by the grace and skill of Alvarito de Villa-Cató's genius, so that the pope could come walking across it, come to the door of Alvarito's house, and give him his blessing. The pope wouldn't be able to resist the temptation of walking on the beautiful carpet. The weaving would seize hold of his feet, not letting him turn back and urging him to go forward. He would come walking all the way from Rome. The angels would provide shade for him by extending their wings during the day, and the fireflies would warm him and light his way at night. It would never rain on the carpet, which, as it unrolled, would seek out the best roads and places with gardens and fruit trees.

"Rest, Alvarito. You're going to get sick. . . ."

"I can't. I'm in a hurry!"

"Alvarito, time to eat!"

"I'll be there as soon as I finish this row. . . ."

"Alvarito, it's almost nighttime!"

"Then light me some candles."

"Alvarito, time to sleep!"

"Later . . . later. . . ."

He died without fulfilling the only goal in his life, and sensing that it was slipping inevitably away from him, he asked to be buried next to his loom.

Lack of exercise had made his body grow just like the carpet, and it was necessary to make a coffin so big that twenty teary-eyed members of the family were needed to carry it.

"It's so heavy!"

"Let's put it on the vegetable wagon!"

"No! That would show a lack of respect, and . . . the mules might crap on the rug. . . ."

To let the cadaver through, the carpet started to unroll, going from the door of Alvarito's room to the door of the church, from the door of the church to the door to the cemetery, then from the door to the cemetery right to the door to his tomb, where it ended.

That's how the city got wall-to-wall carpeting. All of the people in the city helped the family roll out the carpet over the paved streets, moved by curiosity to see where it led to. But once they were satisfied, nobody bothered to put it back where it belonged. Moreover, it was a monster that, having tasted liberty, was impossible to return to its cave after having awakened from hibernation.

"What a marvelous carpet!"

"It's the longest carpet in the world, and they're going to leave it lying in the streets!"

"They can't get it back into the house anymore."

The carpet lay there for five years until the sun and the rain took notice of it. And a few more years went by in which the city was always covered with fuzz balls, which was what the beautiful red carpet had turned into. The wool had faded, and the pink fuzz balls stuck to the black clothing of the people, who were bent under the weight of mourning and *soroche*.

The fuzz balls flew all over whenever the wind blew, getting into the houses through the doors and the bedroom windows. The trees were covered with woolen flowers. The birds were living in a golden age because their nests were softer than ever and even self-decorating. Sometimes the wind blew into the kitchen and people ate soup garnished with fuzz balls.

"What the . . . ?"

"Fuzz balls from the carpet!"

Several more years went by before the fuzz balls disappeared completely. They faded to a faint powder that caused an outbreak of chronic colds. It was a form of "allergy," but that word hadn't been invented yet. . . .

"I've had a cold for four months."

"That's nothing! I've had a cold for a year and a half."

The usual handkerchiefs were replaced with bedsheets. Women's fashions changed. They started wearing enormous pleated skirts that began at the waist and reached to the ankles and required more than ten yards of fabric to make. Beneath these so-called potato sacks, women could carry not only the enormous handkerchiefs needed for their colds, but even the fruits of clandestine love and, if necessary, an entire house.

When the powder got tired of drifting and getting into every nook and cranny, Alvarito's soul also grew tired of drifting to the earth's four corners. Until then his soul had been unable to relax beneath the marble gravestone because he hadn't fulfilled the promise he had made the day of his first communion, and which

86

many people believed in: the pope's arrival in the sleeping city, walking all the way from Rome on the red carpet for whose sake thousands of lambs and sheep had shivered with cold when the magic scissors that helped María Illacatu to exact her vengeance stopped running around the world and cutting up everything that crossed its path. But, as it always turned out, the people's memory of Alvarito was lost to oblivion.

"Who was Alvaro Villa-Cató?"

"A man who rose to become pope."

"How?"

"By walking all the way from here to Rome."

13

Alvarito's younger brother was Jerónimo. Fat, thickheaded, and naive, he used up all the energy that his tremendous appetite gave him raising frogs and toads. This activity allowed him to work off the excess strength that he didn't use up on boring everyday activities.

Work was not something that well-born people did. They couldn't work because they considered work to be humiliating. The hands of white men, and of those who considered themselves to be such, were not made for work because they would be ruined. Jerónimo was incredibly bored; he wandered back and forth, biting his nails and sticking his nose in other people's business, until he came upon the "hobby" that changed his life.

With the exception of Camelia the Tearful, who declared her independence from that environment, the women in Bruna's family were all victims, playthings of their circumstances, due to the cowardice that kept them bound to the men and the self-interest of those men, who never wanted to untie their hands. There was more variety among the men than among the women, whose lives were chained to conventionalisms and who let themselves be influenced by the sickness of *soroche*.

Jerónimo Villa-Cató was the pampered child: he cried inside his mother's belly before he was born, and two days later he was born with a baby tooth as large as a rabbit's. All this indicated that he would be a man who, one way or another, would go down in history and leave the family name in a highly respected position. During his first few years, every little thing he did was considered to be an act of genius and was recorded in a big notebook with green covers. But his life was perfectly ordinary; the only noteworthy thing was his dedication to raising frogs.

The family wanted him to take up painting, but that only resulted in big stains on the floor and the furniture. They thought he would enter history as a saint, but Jerónimo didn't take that path: he bit his nails, rolled his snot into little balls, caught flies in midair, and also liked to climb up the neighbor's wall to peer at their private lives. They wanted to make a Napoleon out of him, but the sound of fireworks scared him, and he would hide under the bed, crying. They tried to introduce him to literature, but he never made it past the second-grade reader. Then they pushed him toward music, thinking that he would follow in Beethoven's footsteps, but he was completely tone deaf. Music bothered him, and he much preferred noises. Also, he had a lot of physical energy: he wasn't the type of man who could sit at a piano keyboard all day. His hearing was totally backward; he preferred hearing the frogs croak to practicing his scales.

"Do, re, mi, fa, sol, la, ti."

"Croak, croak, croak, cr . . ."

At first he kept the frogs in the fountain, but they multiplied so quickly that he had to move them all to a reservoir that he had built for them on the outskirts of the city.

These frog nurseries were sprinkled by giant pumps that imitated the rainfall. He had managed to invent an ingenious apparatus that fooled the frogs. He hung up an immense sheet of tin, and every time he wanted to delight in a concerto he would hit it with a big mallet muffled with rags, and the vibrations produced a perfect series of thunderclaps.

He got up early every day. He ate a big breakfast and would mount his mule right at the dining-room door. The harness and saddle were almost always loose or badly placed. The mule lived at the far end of the garden, eating all the vegetables that it wanted to, as well as the flowers in the beds. The mule and the gentleman left every morning through the big door and didn't come back until six o'clock at night.

He spent the daytime hours opening and closing the water-pump valves so that the frogs would think it was raining and croak, filling the air with music. That was his job. The family let him do it with a mixture of resignation and disappointment, but deep in their hearts they never lost hope that one day he would do something that would go down in history.

The frog nurseries were very large tanks: in the first one, which he called "first pianissimo," he kept the pregnant frogs and fed them daily with the best insects he could find. In another, called "second vivace," were the tadpoles that he grabbed the moment their tails fell off in order to transfer them with all due respect to the one called "third con brio," where they would fulfill their reproductive duties. The tanks were surrounded by chicken wire and stockade fencing to keep the frogs from escaping. They bubbled with repugnant animals who all mingled together, hiding under the immense mats of green scum.

When the tadpoles lost their tails, indicating their maturity, the tails were collected in jars full of water to use as a folk remedy for cleaning and curing eye ailments. The healers would pick up a tail between the thumb and forefinger of their left hand and pass it three times over the crystalline humor of the lens to cure redness, infections, and cataracts.

"Little tail, little tail, by the powers that God has given you, clean this eye of bleariness. . . . Little tail, little tail, by the powers that God has given you, give this poor man back his sight. . . ."

Jerónimo Catovil kept many Indians working day and night shifts at the frog nursery, so that someone would always be keeping an eye on the frogs and nothing unexpected would happen. When one of them died, it was as if Jerónimo were losing a note in the melody that carried him off to heaven. He never heard the news that the legs of his favorite instruments could be eaten and that they were a real delicacy.

"Poor little Jerónimo suffered so much."

"Bah, don't talk to me about that guy!"

"He was my great-uncle. He died relatively young, during the epidemic of—"

"That's a lie! He died of tuberculosis, because he was such a pig!"

To Bruna, Jerónimo was the most degenerate of all her relatives. When she heard about the work he did to keep the tanks in good condition, she shivered with disgust, and no sooner had she recovered than she heard how Jerónimo, already tubercular, never went a single day without seeing his frogs, and how much he walked, sweated, and panted, how the blood refused to keep flowing through his veins, and his lungs were stinging, and he died while spitting them out bit by bit.

When he died, the family forgot about the nursery until one fine day the people saw a green patch appear, slowly approaching the city. Terrorized, they shut their doors and windows, but the frogs paid no attention as they slowly climbed up the walls and roof tiles. The invasion of frogs lasted many months.

"My nerves are shot. Last night, when I was putting on my slippers, my bare foot touched a frog that was hidden there."

"I don't even dare to lie down at night in my own bed out of fear of rubbing against one."

"At breakfast time we were chasing a frog that was about to jump from the lamp to the table. . . ."

"There's going to be a penitential procession tomorrow asking God to deliver us from the frogs."

"Where could so many frogs have come from?"

"They say from the Villa-Catós' house. . . ."

14

The city had many golden churches, the churches had stone plazas, the plazas had bronze monuments, which represented the heroes and worthy men of the city. One of the monuments showed the bishop of Villa-Cató with a book in his right hand and a quill pen in his left that could have just as easily come from a swan or a chicken. Salomón de Villa-Cató was a man who was dedicated to books. It's possible that he was not left-handed. He studied theology in the universities on the other side of the ocean, and he returned, after an absence of many years, bearing a few insignificant gray hairs, beautiful bishop's robes, and an amethyst ring.

Salomón was one of the sons of Jerónimo, who between frogs had his wife and children. If he never led a common, ordinary life, it was because he was always considered to be the child prodigy by his uncles, who died suspecting that the true genius would be Salomón. They urged him to follow a career in the church, sending him very far from the family, and even though they never got to see the monument that was raised to Salomón during his own lifetime, they weren't very far from the truth.

"The inhabitants of this illustrious city erect this monument to this eminent man of faith.—1743—The first day of . . ."

And in smaller letters it read: "(Would that he never die.)"

It was the era when Freemasonry pulled all the political strings in the country. The lives of the city's inhabitants were in their hands. It was believed that the Masons had made a pact with the Devil. It was said that they obeyed dark rules and regulations and that they were responsible for all the crimes committed under the sun, making the pious city dwellers walk on red-hot coals.

Salomón de Villa-Cató realized the danger to his parishioners and, like the bishop that he was, wanted to stop the advancing forces of evil that issued forth from secret meetings that were held in various dark places and were starting to create political ferment.

"Someone has committed an outrage with a young girl!"

"The Freemasons did it. . . ."

"The train from the north has derailed!"

"The Freemasons . . ."

"The rivers have overflowed their banks!"

"It's the Freemasons' fault. . . ."

One morning while the bishop was preparing for his religious offices he came upon his sacristan, who appeared to be nervously trying to hide something as he clumsily set the wine cruets on the silver communion tray. The bishop saw that he had something in his right fist, which even at a distance he knew to be the seeds of death.

"What have you got in your hand?"

"Nothing, nothing . . . most illustrious sir!"

The bishop made him open his hand and saw, to his complete surprise, that it was a small gray envelope, marked with three dots forming a triangle, the signs of evil.

"Jacinto! You traitor! What does this mean?"

"Nothing, nothing . . . most illustrious sir!"

The sacristan was trembling and sweating with fear, and since he would never make an incriminating confession, he swallowed the fatal contents of the envelope himself, hurrying it along with a swallow of holy wine from the cruets and . . . he dropped dead on the spot. The sacristan's rigid corpse and twisted head, with its hair glued to his face, looked just like the sprinkler of holy water and plunged the bishop into deep thought. . . . He soon understood with terror that he was supposed to have been the victim, and not poor Jacinto who was lying at his feet. From that moment on he went on the offensive to save his own hide and the hides of the flock entrusted to him.

The bishop felt cornered. He couldn't trust anyone or anything: even the eye-shaped stitches on the seams of his pillow seemed to be spying on him. He felt that he was being followed and his days were being numbered by sinister men in long black coats and vests. When he broke his bread for breakfast, he was afraid that he would find a small envelope with the fateful three dots on it. He felt he was being watched from the church towers and looked at from every window. The paving stones formed triangular shapes as he walked past. The sparrows flew by in groups of three. The candle flames formed triangles on the altars. Everyone around him seemed to be involved with the sinister sect that day by day seemed to reach its tentacles deeper into the city that, once in their power, would be used as a springboard to world domination. The bishop felt cornered; he didn't even trust his own nephews.

"What should I do, Mother of All Suffering, what should I do? I can't even count on my family; they've been partly touched by this. . . ."

So he hatched a plan that only a Catovil could have come up with: he moved into the foundling home at the edge of his bishopric and started peopling it with boys whom he indoctrinated, from the moment they learned the alphabet—which he taught them himself—with a blinding hatred for the sacrilegious sect.

All the boys looked alike and thought alike. They were nursed on goat's milk and pills to counter the ill effects of *soroche*. From early on they were hardy, robust, and alert, and none of them were more than five years old, which was how long it took to make them that way. The first part of the scheme took five years, and everything went exactly according to plan. They all had the same last name because they were all children of the same father, and in addition, they were produced by the choicest selection of women who weren't contaminated by the sect, which was easy to find out from his dealings with the women who went frequently to confession.

The first part of the plan started to unfold rather slowly. The future mothers collaborated gladly with the bishop, and for five years they did nothing but deliver baby boys to the bishop's foundling house, boys who would eventually wipe all disgrace from the face of the earth.

At first, the husbands felt a terrible sensation of being cuckolded; but when they realized that they weren't the only ones, and that their wives were otherwise completely faithful, and the bishop intervened to assure them that their wives were purer than polished communion trays, they got used to the idea.

After twenty years the foundling house had become a disciplined barracks. Two hundred and forty-five brothers obeyed only the orders of their father and commander in chief, Villa-Cató. They had received highly polished educations, and their knowledge of culture was very broad indeed. All of the bishop's knowledge was emptied into them, and there had never been a captain prouder of his battalion than he was. They formed a religious and military order that was inspired by the knights of the Crusades. When they received their first commands and the rank of lieutenant, they were designated with the name the Battalion of Faith.

"How gallant, how well groomed, how valiant our sons are!"

"But they never look at a woman, not even their own mothers."

"We can't even go near them. . . ."

"It's all in the name of religion!"

They were 245 knights-errant. In their first sortie against the enemy, they sowed terror among the liberal armies, behind which the murky forces of evil were hiding.

The Battalion of Faith was invincible; inferior in numbers to every one of the armies that they clashed with in more than one hundred confrontations, they never had a casualty worth mentioning. Just the name "the Battalion of Faith" made its enemies tremble.

The battle of ideals moved into the family sphere, putting the battlefield with its ambushes and cannon fire right in the heart of every home, because practically everyone was a sympathizer, on the father's side with the Freemasons and on the mother's side with the Battalion of Faith.

The small number of women who couldn't fulfill their part of the bargain by producing male children had to take care of the girls, who were permitted to keep their fathers' names and received economic assistance when they needed it.

Everyone knew that the Battalion of Faith was made up of the sons of Salomón de Villa-Cató. This fact was not hidden, because their father had not engendered them out of lust, or for crooked reasons, but as part of a larger strategy, which was entirely different. . . . The conservative faction of the city got used to seeing these soldiers as champions and defenders of their dearest beliefs. The bishop could walk the streets of the city with his head held high and pose with pride so that they could erect, during his own life, the great monument that graced the plaza. The mothers were proud of their fertile bellies because they had contributed to the formation of a race of heroes and saints.

For reasons of discipline, and because the *Book of Saints* was insufficient for his taste, the bishop saw the need to number all the children he was producing. Sons and daughters all had their corresponding Christian numbers very carefully registered.

"My oldest daughter isn't a Sánchez, she's a Villa-Cató."

"I see. What's her number?"

"She's María the Seventeenth."

"My third daughter is María the Fourteenth."

"Well, I didn't know that our daughters were sisters."

"Neither did I."

The Battalion of Faith became world famous. Its exploits crossed over the mountains and swam the seas. It was an indestructible army. Their final act was giving the sinister sect a death blow right smack in their honor. The chief of the Masons, Don Manuel Benavides, thirty-third grade, was dying in his own bed. His wife was in the opposite faction, and she took advantage of the situation to convince him that it was urgent and necessary to go to the great beyond with his conscience lightened so that the trip would be shorter and to avoid last-minute surprises. She called for a priest, who came to hear number 33's confession. No sooner had the priest appeared at the bedside than someone warned the venerable brothers of the Great Orient who were gathered around the dying man, but he had already cast out everything that was inside him. The wife told the Battalion of Faith what was going on at the very borderline between life and death, and the whole battalion marched on the dying man's house. As soon as the brothers of the Great Orient heard the tramping of soldiers' boots only a few feet away, they thought there was going to be a battle. They fled, leaving the semicadaver in the hands of the priest, who in proper fashion removed the weight from the suffering man's conscience, made a neat little package out of what he had been told, and left with it. Don Manuel Benavides lay there livid, stiff, and lightened.

"Don Manuel confessed, Don Manuel confessed!"

"With who, tell me with who?"

"With some priest who happened by. . . ."

The bishop of Villa-Cató burned with desire to know the contents of the package, but the priest was bound by the secrecy of the confessional and would not deliver it into his superior's hands, and to avoid the temptation of opening the package, he carried it up the city's volcano. After two days he reached the crater, threw the entire contents of the package down into its steaming jaws, and returned greatly relieved to his normal duties.

But the volcano, which tormented the pious city dwellers every afternoon with its rumblings and quakings, got even more steamed up from the bothersome package, and, shaking violently, it began spewing out a rain of ash for forty nights that blocked out the sun and covered the city with a thick layer of foreboding and panic.

"The volcano's going to erupt!"

"There's going to be an earthquake!"

"It's all the Freemasons' fault!"

Tired of so much squabbling, the Freemasons resolved once and for all to retaliate and thought up a way of exterminating the Battalion of Faith. After many trials and subterfuges they managed to infiltrate their very headquarters; and with threats and bribery they caught the cook.

The ash kept falling. The bishop didn't rest for a minute. The city folk begged and promised. The Battalion of Faith gave up their advanced theological studies and polished their swords in their free time.

And so it happened that when the Day of Resurrection came, the 245 soldiers were hungrier than ever owing to prolonged fasting during the forty days of Lent. The cook, as instructed, served out 245 portions of vitriol sulfate in the thick and foamy cocoa. One by one, the valiant defenders of the faith sipped the cocoa and fell face-down right there at the dining-room table.

"They killed the soldiers of the faith!"

"They poisoned them!"

"Revenge! Revenge!"

"They killed our sons!"

The bishop cried for his sons, sons of his violent flesh and his warring spirit. For eight days the bells of the city rang, awakening with their sad pealing the souls of the dead who slept in their tombs. The volcanic earthquakes grew in strength, and the ash fell heavier than ever. The city fell into the hands of the forces of evil, but the Freemasons were so discredited that they couldn't seize the moment to act. The women made their lives impossible, so much so that many of them could be seen going to church to take part in the penitential processions. The women went into mourning for two years. They hung black ribbons and crepe from the iron bars in the windows. The city sank into silence: the wagon drivers wrapped their wheels with rags to keep them from making noise against the paving stones. Children tiptoed around inside their houses, and even the street vendors stopped hawking their wares.

Salomón de Villa-Cató quit being a bishop and, wearing a worn cassock, started walking in the direction of sunrise. He walked alone for many years, eating the bitter roots of trees and wild fruits, drinking the rainwater that collected in rocks and in the stems of *penco* cactuses. He crossed the farthest mountains and reached the place where María Illacatu was born, where he found shadows, ruins, and a solitude that was somehow familiar to him. . . .

When she was a little girl, Bruna thought that the exploits of the Battalion of Faith were just another of the many legends from the old days, but one afternoon when she was wandering around the back rooms of the big old house she tripped on a pile of old iron. She climbed onto a trunk and opened a window, and an oblique shaft of light revealed a pile of rusted swords. She counted them, and in fact there were 245. . . .

"Mama Chana, whose swords are in that room?"

"I told you, they belonged to the bishop's sons."

"Tell me again."

"All right. Many years ago, when . . ."

15

Salomón de Villa-Cató's few daughters were lost in anonymity. One of them was known to all of the Villa-Catós by the name of María the Twenty-third. She was born to a well-dressed matron already fairly advanced in years who didn't know what to do with her, and since having a daughter did not fit in with her plans and the girl wasn't the product of a marriage anyway, she was sent to the countryside, where she grew up with the simplicity of the onions and the honesty of the turnips. She married a young man who was also the secret nephew of one of Camelia the Tearful's maiden aunts. The two young people came from the same family tree, but from different branches, and although their parents didn't want them around while they were alive, they remembered them in their wills, and that's how they suddenly became the owners of a great deal of property that they didn't know what to do with or how to run.

The two of them lived with each other from the time they were children and grew up without knowing how to read or write. When somebody told them that they were old enough to get married—since they knew of no other candidates—they decided to marry each other, and once they were married they prepared to visit the city for the first time.

"When we get married, we'll go see the city."

"We'll see the houses that are built on top of each other. . . ."

"And all lined up in rows. . . ."

"We'll see tall churches made of pure gold."

"We'll meet all our relatives."

When they went to the city, they arrived at the big family house and met with surprise after surprise. They became engrossed in wondering how water could squeeze itself past the little mermaid's tiny waist in the courtyard fountain. They saw how the houses had one floor on top of another and thought that to build such tall churches they must have had to move the mountains closer and then, once construction was finished, move them back again. They were astonished to learn that it was possible to capture a ray of sunlight in a glass jar and hang it from a rope to light up the night. They were left speechless by the machines for measuring time and stood there stunned at the doorway to the bathroom.

What caught their attention the most was an enormous white cup that—they were told—was used for bodily needs. The city folk didn't relieve themselves on the ground, as they had done since time immemorial in the countryside, but rather in this well-defined apparatus that, furthermore, was made of porcelain. They liked the invention so much that they spent the two weeks of their honeymoon taking turns sitting on the device, then flushing the water to see and hear the "trolop" sound in the bottom of the cup and how, by magic, all traces of filth and bad smells disappeared.

"Look, look at it go!"

"Where does it go to?"

"They say to the sea."

"The sea must be full of garbage."

When they returned to the countryside they brought a whole storeful of these fabulous devices. They also brought a specialist to install them in the ranch house and in the Indians' huts as well. When the specialist went back to the city, even the farm animals knew how to use them.

Even though they couldn't read, María the Twenty-third and her husband had a vague idea about how to use money. It seemed unfair that just because they were white, only they could participate in the city's progress, and not the Indians who worked from sun to sun to increase their wealth. They hated flies, not for reasons of hygiene—which nobody had ever told them about—but because of their buzzing and appearance. Then they got very uncomfortable when, after walking hand in hand around their extensive property, and watching how the wheat grew, how the corn developed, and how the cows reproduced, after returning from seeing such marvels, they got back to the house with their shoes so dirty and smelly that they had to throw them in the garbage. Soon the garbage pails were filled with unmatched shoes, and sometimes they had to wear shoes of different colors, styles, and quality, until the peddlers came by selling sugar, soap, cloth, and shoes.

"I'm sick of stepping in so much shit!"

"Me too."

"There aren't any sturdy shoes, or soles that last!"

The work on the hacienda went along smoothly, filling the sheds with grain and the coffers with money. But when hygienic methods were introduced, things started to go bad. The Indian population was decimated.

The masters had prohibited the one thousand Indians who lived on the hacienda, along with their wives and children, from attending to their bodily needs on the face of the earth. The penalty for disobeying the order was a whipping. The overseer of the hacienda spent a week announcing it:

"Fifty lashes on the buttocks for an adult and twenty-five lashes on the buttocks for a child if you attend to your needs in the open, in the fields, in the ditches, or in the pastures, and not in the cups that the masters have given you."

At first a few had to be whipped as examples, but soon you could take a carefree walk around the countryside.

"Now it's a pleasure to go for a walk."

"The earth smells like earth, and the flowers like flowers."

However, the process began to affect them internally. The country air began to fill with vapors just like the ones in the city that produced *soroche*. It wasn't pure air anymore, but the end result of fear, frustration, and repressed desires. The Indians were very docile and submissive and wanted to please their masters, but they couldn't, and that inability cost them their lives. . . .

After a while they all died of intestinal miseries. Their bodies, which were used to being in a certain position for a certain act, wouldn't adjust to the change. Sitting on the cups was like sitting in the clouds, coming in contact with the cold rim and the darkness at the bottom made them feel like the master was watching them from underneath and so . . . they couldn't. Although the will and desire to obey was strong, the ability was weak. They wanted to, but they couldn't. . . .

"No can, master, no can."

"Push all day, still no can."

One by one all the Indians on the hacienda died. Sadly and painfully, they met their ends in the same manner—although not, as they say, with the same ideas—as Voltaire did.

The folk healers and witch doctors cast all kinds of spells on the strange devices that the masters had ordered everyone to use, but nothing helped. They died in the grips of violent convulsions, their eyes dumbfounded with panic because they had disobeyed, with their orifice of elimination completely inverted, with strange pains and contortions that nobody had ever suffered, all the time thinking that this was how it had to be, that there was no other way. . . .

When the last Indian was buried, María the Twenty-third and her husband understood that they had gone too far. They emptied the coffers of money, saddled up all the mules they needed with their personal effects, and set out for the city. They traveled without saying a word, deep in thought, thinking that what had happened was the same as if one day someone had decided to force the two of them to try to sleep standing up, with their arms in the air, trying to reach the stars and grab hold of the moon to use it as a pillow.

Once in the city, they bought the house next door to their relatives and tried to live the way people there lived. They found a tutor to teach them how to read and write. It was touching to see them hold out their right hand for a caning from the tutor when their homework wasn't done properly. They filled thousands of pages with calligraphy, learned the four basic arithmetic operations, a little religious history and geography, they memorized Carreño's *Guide to Manners,* and at the end of a relatively short time they realized that the tutor no longer had anything to teach them and they dismissed him. Then, after ten years of marriage, they started to have children, because—in spite of living in the countryside and seeing the daily coupling of animals—they were so naive that they did not know what humans did to get children. . . . This extraordinary couple gave birth to Bruna.

16

Camelia the Tearful died six years after she left the convent for her failed role as a mother. When the newest batch of two nieces and one nephew were left alone again, they started to take care of themselves, led by the eldest, Catalina. The three children were the worst thing that happened to Camelia the Tearful, but in spite of what she transmitted to them from her awful time period, they still managed to surpass her in manias and complexes.

Francisco José, who was the middle child, grew to be a tall, dapper, elegant man. During the nine months of his gestation, his mother spent hours and hours doing nothing but looking at a scrapbook with portraits of princes and princesses from Charlemagne's family tree.

"Our brother Francisco is so handsome!"

"You'd think he was a count or a duke. . . . Our mother didn't spend all that time with the scrapbook on her knees for nothing!"

The sisters talked about geraniums, cats, embroidery, saints' lives, things the city folk did, and their brother's eyes: they said they were green, or blue, when in fact they were as yellow as the skin of a leopard. His thick eyebrows nearly joined together on his forehead, giving him a ferocious appearance, and a few extra-long and powerful hairs stood out from the crowd: they seemed to belong not to him but rather to some giant, which made his eyes the center of attraction of his face.

"Francisco's eyes are green, they're green. . . ."

"But Catalina, they look blue to me. . . ."

"Then you can't see clearly."

For them and the rest of the family, Uncle Francisco was the most important man in the city. His importance derived in part from his large library, where he stayed shut in for hours on end, placing between himself and his relations an impassable barrier of culture, which for the most part took shape in his brilliant writings, thanks to a general epilepsy of ultrarefined and distinguished words that flowed out torrentially and twisted around like a nest of earthworms holding a few loose ideas.

He spoke very little and only to certain select people, underlining with his eyebrows the few words that he deigned to utter from time to time. So the hairs moved up and down like a crab's claws, following the rhythm of an accusing finger. They looked like Dalí's mustache.

The aunts supposed that inspiration came to him through his eyebrows when he sat down to compose his verses, but—for the sake of truth—that was really where idiocy flowed out of him when he was busy with his favorite pastime, which was collecting empty matchboxes, a mania on which he remained fixated his entire life.

As the years went by, his wavering mental balance lost all stability. From time to time he wrote verses, trying to continue the tradition of the brilliant world that Camelia the Tearful opened herself up to, before messing up his destiny by giving himself over to an absurd love. When he was young he fell in love with the daughter of the city's match manufacturer, who was a European immigrant; that was when he dedicated himself with true frenzy to poetry, which seemed to replace, for a while, his mania of collecting matchboxes.

"What, our brother goes around with matches? No, no, that's a vicious lie! He is a poet of high, of the highest caliber. . . ."

Everything was fine, at first, among his narrow circle of friends, since he was a man of letters and his sisters made sure, for as long as they could, that his mania didn't get beyond the oak doors of the house, and they took charge of spreading the word about his literary talent to the four winds. His name appeared in one contemporary anthology after another. But time itself wiped the slate clean, since the results looked like this:

> *Pensil florido*
> *Rosicler plúmbeo*
> *Cual idolatro, aura doncella;*
> *Todo el que otea, fenece al verla:*
> *Su cabellera argentadora;*
> *Siendo luceros bajo las cejas*
> *Filis querube . . . Muera Satán. . . .*

> Hanging garden
> Leaden pink of dawn
> Which idolater, gentle maid;
> All those who search, expire upon seeing her:
> Her silvery hair;
> With bright stars below her eyebrows
> Cherubic charm . . . Satan dies. . . .

Bruna despaired over her uncle's verses, which she had to read every afternoon at her aunts' insistence.

"I understand nothing, nothing!"

"That's because your head is full of sawdust."

But the sisters continued to ponder his writings, which they never understood either, because women weren't supposed to understand poetry; and in that way they tried desperately to draw the city folks' attention to his words and cover up the business with the matchboxes. They never admitted that their brother, Francisco, was nothing but a crazy collector of garbage.

"Francisco's verses have been praised abroad."

"They've crossed the ocean!"

"Those who know say he is the most important poet in the city."

"And they don't just say it, they put it in writing!"

17

The house was divided according to the principle of one floor per adult. Because of the unevenness of the ground, the third floor had the most rooms, and that was where Uncle Francisco lived with his matchboxes. The floor had sixteen big rooms with identical doors and identical windows.

The rooms were big, of the same proportions as Uncle Francisco's eyebrows. The incredibly high ceilings were lost in a cloud of cobwebs and suppositions. They said that since polluted air was denser than pure air, the ceilings needed to be very high in order for "the carbonics" to be farther from people's lungs. But no one knew about "carbonics" until many years later, because in the old days they said that it was the foul humors of bad intentions; and so that the children would see that what their uncles said was true, one of them took a lit candle and climbed up on a chair and put the candle on top of a cupboard, and the candle was instantly snuffed out, which demonstrated beyond all doubt that what the uncles said was true.

The walls were wide and one meter thick because they had to resist the brutal onslaught of constant tremors that kept making the people in the peaceful city dizzy. Over the mud walls they had glued beautiful sheets of wallpaper of the most unpredictable variety of patterns that made for the most delightful, fitful sleep and was good for those moments when the parties went on and on and there was nothing left to talk about, leading to those interminable silences in which each person feels guilty.

"Nobody's saying anything. . . . What should I say?"

"I'm so ashamed. . . . What horrible silence!"

"My God, somebody say something!"

"Let's see who speaks first. . . ."

The wallpaper in Uncle Francisco's library depicted a seascape where enormous bluish herons relaxed and sunbathed in a row, alternately kissing the beak or the tail of its neighbor while standing on one foot in the habitual manner of herons. Their feathers were reflected in the pond water, which was covered with lotus leaves. But the watery mirror, returning their upside-down images, forgot about the hidden leg and displayed herons with both feet sticking straight up and none in reserve, which plunged all the spectators, Bruna among them, into deep thought about the reality of the things that we see that aren't really so. It was an unreality that became even more complex when Bruna first put on her school uniform, which was a white pinafore with her name on it in big red letters, and when she saw herself in the mirror she couldn't read her name because it was backward:

"What do people see? How do they see? Which is the reality? Is the truth in our eyes, in other people's eyes, in the mirror's reflection? . . ."

It was also said:

"Could it be that water, being water, can reflect dark and hidden things, like the eye of the Devil down in the well?"

The library with the herons and the uncle's bedroom, wallpapered in a pastel blue depicting two-wheeled carriages that were once gilded, in which beautiful ladies traveled nowhere, were the only rooms that Bruna had seen on the third floor. The others always had both their doors and windows locked, protecting the oversize collection of matchboxes.

Uncle Francisco's fondness for the little boxes began when he was a little boy learning how to crawl around the floor, which was covered with a green cloth to protect them from the cold bricks. Francisco wanted something, and nobody knew what it was, so he had a tantrum that drove Aunt Camelia the Tearful crazy—she had just left the convent. She opened a cupboard to shove the screaming Francisco inside, and everything spilled out. Francisco shut up as if by magic, taken by the surprise of what he saw on the floor: empty bottles of perfume, tiny silver spoons, bits of colored ribbon, balls of wool, and countless empty matchboxes, which he immediately grabbed, charting his destiny from that moment on. He held on to the matchboxes as if they were a treasure; he played all day with them and then slept with them, and they got all smeared with the watery porridge that the serving maids ate.

The family gave him more and more matchboxes, amazed to see how thrilled the boy was to receive them and how well behaved he became, before putting them away for safekeeping. He soon needed a whole cupboard just to hide them from the zealous brooms. Aunt Camelia apprehensively let him have it after another tantrum. He gradually gave up the handmade spinning tops, soccer balls, and his sisters' rag dolls that he had been playing with up until then and continued to warehouse more and more matchboxes as he grew up.

In the full bloom of youth he tried to sublimate his mania for collecting matchboxes from different countries of the world, but it hurt him to throw out the little boxes his aunt the ex-nun had given him, because they were the friends he never had as a child, or because of their bright colors in spite of the layer of dirt that covered them, and he applied himself to collecting without rhyme or reason. He was a hardened sentimentalist.

Years went by, and nobody could change Uncle Francisco's mind. He had decreed that the house stopped at the second floor. Since these decisions came from a man of letters, everyone got used to accepting his harebrained opinions as if they were absolute and irrefutable laws. They got used to living in a house with two floors and to believing that their uncle lived in the clouds. On the stairs leading to the third floor was a white cardboard sign with black India ink letters that read:

"It is categorically prohibited for members of this household and for visitors alike to make any momentary or sustained movement toward my private rooms, constituted and situated from this point upward."

An old Indian, deaf and bent double under the weight of his sad past—carried not in his eyes, like some other Indians, but on his shoulders—was able to reach the third floor by walking on the uncle's command and on the soles of his own feet, which were thicker than the soles of the shoes that the people in the house wore. Only he, with his rags and broom, cleaned up there from time to time to prevent the spread of the many rats that were there in spite of Aunt Clarita's six cats.

The first two rooms were kept in some kind of order. The matchboxes were lined up along the walls until they reached the ceiling and came forward until they reached the exact spot where the doors could be closed. Later on he didn't even take this amount of care; he piled up the matchboxes until they disappeared out of sight, and when the doors wouldn't budge anymore he shoved them in through a crack until there wasn't room for a single one more.

Then he shut the rooms with the intention of never opening them again. It was impossible to enter them without destroying a large portion of his valuable collection: if he had been hoarding gold, he would have been the richest man in the city; if he had been collecting jewelry, he would have robbed all the women of the world of their tools of the trade; if he had been collecting children, he would have populated an entire continent. . . .

When he was finished with one room he started preparing another: he removed the furniture that had been deposited in the back rooms of the house, regardless of whether it had sentimental or monetary value, or was still useful, and it soon was eaten by worms and rats. Then he started over, with the same energy and drive as when he first took over the house that he considered to be the property of the matchboxes.

Nobody entered the back rooms of the house because of the smell left behind where the imps relieved themselves. That's where it all turned to dust: the old furniture that belonged to María Illacatu and her children, the delicate furniture upon which Camelia the Tearful gathered the quintessence of thought and intellectualism in the sleeping city, the fourteen sad children's shirts, María the Twenty-third's farming tools . . . The back rooms of the house were a compost heap of memories and the place where one could find the words that were missing from the archives and the truth about the family history. The little mermaid lay on her side in a corner, forgotten, feeling the spiders' hairy legs as they walked across her beautiful naked body, shivering with disgust, cold, and shame, sighing for some clothing, for the water of the fountain, and for the air of the faraway patio. . . .

18

Uncle Francisco José died years earlier, but he kept accumulating matchboxes. Almost every time the enormous piles of matchboxes collapsed, Uncle Francisco's skeleton gave a shudder and left his tomb, no matter what day, month, or year or what condition he or anyone else was in. The way the matchboxes collapsed was comparable only to the despair of a living man of flesh and blood, of moods and fears, when he has missed the last bus home and has to spend a rainy night sitting between the headstones in a cemetery, where so many unforeseen things can occur; or the despair of a woman bathing in the river who suddenly realizes that the current is carrying her clothes away. . . .

News of the uncle's mania spread through the city—as if it were the shocking story of a virgin being raped, with all its scandalous details—in spite of the infinite precautions that his sisters took; to them, he would always be sitting at his writing desk, creating the most inspired verses that would make the family name immortal.

"They say that old man Catovil has twelve million matchboxes."

"Crazy old man!"

"All the Catovils are like that."

The city contributed to burying the uncle under an avalanche of matchboxes. More and more matchboxes kept arriving.

"You know something? A new box full of matches costs two and a half centavos and old man Catovil pays five centavos for the empty ones."

"You think I don't know? I've been selling them to him for years. . . ."

The matchboxes' place of origin extended all the way to hell, where some of the packages came from, carefully sealed and addressed to the uncle with a piece of calcified finger bone, along with the full amount for return postage: carefully included in the envelope was some paper money and a sigh.

The traveling peddlers and garbage collectors were always talking about what happened when they pulled the doorbell rope. The uncle, who in life had appeared to be so meticulous, would come flying down the stairs, or skiing down a ray of light, with his shirt thrown over his skeleton and shaving cream on his faceless skull, with his pants half on, and sometimes with his private parts covered by nothing more than a bit of haste that the wind blew away; this scared the visitors, but they always came back.

At this time the fleeting infatuation with the one he called his lady love in his verses ended, because the one time she wanted to give him a kiss, she discovered, to her sheer terror, that her hands went through the man's face, that he wasn't so much a body as a shadow that walked and talked and must have had the power to walk through closed doors and the meter-thick walls.

"Don't leave me alone with him!"

"He's going to be your husband. . . ."

"I'd rather die!"

"He has respect, money, and a name. . . ."

"I'm entering a convent tomorrow!"

More years went by, and his death began when the matchboxes started to come tumbling down and he, suspended in the void, had to bend down, pick up the matchboxes that were hiding between the bones of his hand, and pile them back up; some stayed where they were supposed to, but the majority fell down again, bringing down with them those that had been restacked. He spent an eternity this way, alternating between night and death, with his heart shriveled up and dried out, changed into an empty box hanging between the matchsticks of his ribs.

Once he had lost all sense of time, he lost all sense of order and started to toss them around by the shovelful, helped along by the long hairs of his eyebrows, which had changed into two extra arms. The bats also helped him out with their wings. The sun stopped shining for him, and the earth stopped quaking; his sisters also died—perhaps, he thought, from old age—or maybe they got lost forever while wandering in the back rooms of the house, or on the other side of the orchard, or had fallen into the hands inside the well. . . . His nieces and nephews had vanished, victims of measles or smallpox, or maybe they were still alive. . . . His old school friends had been wiped out in one of the many revolutions between the liberals and the conservatives. . . . The city's church bells had fallen silent: they didn't call anyone to Mass or toll for the dead. Saturdays, February, and Christmas had disappeared forever, while the fish on the fountain vomited up its colorless, liquid laugh, laughing at the uncle and his labors. . . .

At night, kindly Aunt Clarita put ice-cold compresses on the part of his body where his kidneys were supposed to be.

"Rest a little, my dear brother, you're killing yourself!"

"Matches . . . matches . . ."

"Every day you get thinner, I can count your ribs."

"Matches . . . matches . . ."

Aunt Catalina shook her head while saying the rosary and looked away every time the compresses were changed so as not to see the transparent flesh in such a strategic and masculine part of the body. Mama Chana boiled some corn silk in water and give it to him to drink. They opened the curtains and fumigated the room with three coals lit from the flame from the Devil's sneeze, which they had managed to capture on the eve of All Saints' Day. They sprinkled the coals with three grains of aluminum sulfate and three pinches of sugar so that the spirit that was tormenting the man of the house would leave his body; it did, resting for a moment under the tile eaves, then came back to be alone with him.

But Uncle Francisco spent whole nights unable to shut his eyes, calculating how many matchboxes there were in the world, and the distances and times involved that would bring them under his control, and all the roads, mountains, and seas that he'd have to cross, and the risks that he'd have to run before returning home.

So that this dead man who moved around so much could finally rest and leave the living in peace, they decided to hold his funeral before he became completely rigid.

"They say old man Catovil is dying!"

"The one with the matchboxes? I thought he died years ago. . . ."

Meanwhile, his sisters didn't realize (through no fault of their own) that the old man, on his deathbed, had married none other than Mama Chana. They were too occupied with making sure that he left for the great beyond with all due provisions, and with the appropriate baggage, to realize that they were present at the wedding that was celebrated right under their noses. The dead man put his shaky signature on a document that the sacristan presented him with; he was ignorant of its contents—since he was ignorant of everything—as were his sisters, who were unbelievably busy anointing him with oil, and it said that Mama Chana's children, who were quite numerous, were the children of Don Francisco Catovil. In addition, they were now recognized before the laws of God and man as genuine children, children he had nothing to do with, or if he did, he didn't realize what he was doing at the time. . . .

The aunts, horrified by Mama Chana's audacity, threw her out of the house. They sprinkled holy water in all the rooms, chanted psalms in the long hallways, folded the tablecloths that were spread out on the table so that the angels wouldn't cry, since there was already plenty of reason for them to cry. They paid the debts to the unknown senders of matchboxes. They were in extremely complicated mourning for ten years. They cried for their brother, who was the man of the house, the moral endorsement of their customs and of their respective virginities, and each one died convinced that throwing the treacherous Mama Chana out into the street put an end to everything, and that of all the family stories only the house remained, to be inherited by the nephews who had no other possessions besides their family name, four prejudices, and many confused memories in a trunk full of useless things.

One week before the uncle died, the whole third floor caught fire, with all sixteen rooms full of matchboxes. It was a spectacular fire, a major event in the life of the city. The firemen, always vigilant, faultlessly fulfilled their role by letting the whole third floor burn up—which was the secret desire of all sensible people and of those whose job it was to maintain order—and they managed to bring the scourge under control at precisely the moment before the flames consumed the rest of the house and spread to the neighbors' houses. It was a display of true precision and mastery for which they were greatly praised.

The one who set the fire was Bruna.

19

In the school where Bruna studied the two plus two of how the world was created in seven days, the perpetual problem of Adam's apple, the past perfect tense of all possible and impossible human actions, they had every Thursday off. That day the nieces and nephews got together to visit their aunts and uncle, arriving at the house in groups starting from the early morning on. They had noon dinner with them: stew, fried meat with vegetables from the garden, sugary empanadas, and orgeat syrup with milk. They went to the orchard and gathered the fallen fruit from under the leafy cherry tree, and as they chewed and their teeth bit down on the round pits, they felt as if the trees, their aunts and uncle, the eye of the Devil in the bottom of the well, and everything else that surrounded them left a taste of bitter almonds. . . .

They made molasses in the enormous kitchen, and when they put their lime-soaked hands in the thick syrup, they had fun stirring and stirring, making shapes until the syrup became as thick and smooth as wax. Then they started to eat it and ate so much that they felt a dry burning in their throats that was relieved only when they cupped their hands to drink from the fountain, splashing their faces with water.

"Don't eat so many sweets, you'll get a stomachache," said Aunt Clarita.

"It's the sin of gluttony," added Aunt Catalina, *caca de gallina*.

Later on they helped bathe the cats, which was the big event of the day.

"*Caramba,* it's Thursday!"

"No school and we get to bathe the cats! Hooray! Hooray!"

Thursdays were holidays, a pivotal part of their childhood, a whole universe with the sun, moon, and stars all mixed together in the old family house. Bathing the cats was the spectacle that substituted for the circus that never came to the sleeping city. The garden with the eye of the Devil that could never be clogged up by throwing in pebbles and clods of earth from a safe distance away and the imps who looked down from the tile roof were the entryway into a friendly and mysterious world of legend and fantasy.

The fire happened on a Thursday. The blaze broke out during lunch, while they were serving the stew, which was tasteless, and unleashed its full fury before they reached dessert. The youngest nephews flew out of the house to watch it from the neighboring house, where they lived, and didn't come back because they had a feeling that they wouldn't be bathing the cats that day. The other nieces and nephews left one at a time, pretending that they were just going to have a look outside, so the adults remained ignorant of the true extent of the fire. Only Bruna stayed with Aunt Clarita.

"Holy God! Today is Thursday . . . and the children, the cats, and now this conversation, which is getting worse and worse!"

The aunts and the uncle generally lived a calm life that was broken only on Thursdays by the presence of the nieces and nephews, who never stopped hearing the wailing of the ghosts; that day their uncle's phantom bumped into things more often, and the water from the fountain flowed more noisily and generously.

The aunts and the uncle got along well, as all people do who live together and have nothing to say to each other. They talked about superficial and uninteresting things that were worth less than silence and that had no more significance or usefulness than gymnastic tongue exercises. They talked about how the food tasted, the weather, of little scandals that resulted from people taking the pills to

119

counteract *soroche,* and of a series of events that were the same in all the houses in the city. The nieces and nephews listened to long sermons about purity, the dangers of easy living and laziness, and how to be well behaved, especially when visiting someone else's house.

"Don't put your elbows on the table."

"Laziness is the mother of all vices."

"One should use only three-quarters of a chair to sit on."

"God knows our most intimate thoughts."

"Don't slurp your soup."

"What does it serve a man to gain the whole world if he loses his soul?"

"You have to wait until the adults begin eating first."

"We are never alone, we have a guardian angel."

"You must dry your lips with a napkin after drinking water."

The two aunts took care of their brother's health, suggesting to him with a prudence that bordered on fear that he already had enough matchboxes, to which he barely grunted his responses:

"Dear brother Francisco, you have so many. . . . That's enough. . . ."

"Grrr!"

The verbal gymnastics took place at mealtime, when everyone was together, because it seemed as if the food didn't go down right if it wasn't helped along with words. On Thursdays the meal was even longer, slower, and more ceremonious than the other days of the week because the uncle had decided that if he didn't chew properly, the nieces and nephews would notice that his skin was transparent and might be able to see his digestive processes through his clothes. He ate cautiously, making a show of good manners. He unfolded his napkin, shaking it violently so that the ghosts that were hidden within its folds wouldn't get into his mouth when he wiped his lips. He took this precaution because on more than one occasion the ghosts had gotten inside his stomach and would come back out again at the most inopportune times, and the vibrations caused the piles of matchboxes to come tumbling down in the same manner and following the same physical laws as when the Israelites made the walls of Jericho come tumbling down by blowing their trumpets.

That day, when the family sat down at the dinner table, the sisters tried to send the food in the right direction by reminding the uncle that he hadn't written any verses in a thousand years:

"Dear brother Francisco, we've been deprived of your verses for the longest time. . . ."

"No! And on that subject, let me tell you that . . ."

The atmosphere became unbreathable, it was so full of chemicals and bad omens. Suddenly there was talk not about verses, but about matches. There were even matchsticks in the soup. It was as if a thick, bluish smoke were climbing up their legs.

"What? You want the sewing room for your matchboxes?"

"That's it, that's the one, and the room next to it also."

"What? You're coming down to the second floor?"

"Yes! And I want them emptied out now, quickly. . . . I don't have any more room for anything!"

"Never!"

"What? But . . . to me? . . ."

The uncle took over two more rooms on the second floor. He had finished with the third floor, and he was still alive. . . . The storm raging at the dining-room door slipped under their chairs along with its thunder and lightning.

The rooms that the uncle took over were the so-called sewing room, in which no one ever sewed a single stitch, except for Camelia the Tearful's mother when she started embroidering shirts for each one of the fourteen children she brought into the world, to keep from dying of boredom; and the room where Aunt Clarita gathered with her nieces and nephews to read *The Perfect Girls* by the countess of Ségur or *Lord Chesterfield's Letters to his Children* and *El Peneca* (the children's magazine), but most of all where they gathered during the long season of Lent to listen to their aunts give boring lectures about the lives of the saints.

All the nieces and nephews hated saintliness because they associ-

121

ated it with stupidity: the legend of Ramayana—a tiger among men—single-handedly destroying an army of fourteen thousand men was as hard to swallow as that of Palemon of Estilita, who stood for forty years, out of love of God, on a pillar in the middle of the desert. . . . The saint's balancing act on top of the column, and Saint Rose of Lima making a pact with the mosquitoes not to bite her, and their echoing her with buzzing while she played her pious songs on the guitar, seemed pretty stupid compared with Little Red Riding Hood talking to a wolf and betting on who would get to grandmother's house first. Between the female saints who ripped open their own flesh and from whose blood white lilies sprung forth, and the male saints who lay down on beds of thorns to defeat temptation, while the Devil bit his tail in anger, the children had a tough time learning anything but boredom. They never dared to say that the saints were unpleasant because they were cold, distant, and did horrible things, while their other heroes were friendly and worthy of imitation because they did gracious or marvelous things that fed their imaginations and fantasies.

Bruna was enjoying herself thinking about the stories that nourished her childhood, so she didn't hear which precise word caused the storm to break out. Aunt Catalina—*caca de gallina*—and Uncle Francisco José, the one with the matchboxes, were yelling at each other. It was a rare event in the old house. They said terrible things to each other, most of them avoiding the point. They were like the boilers of a train getting ready to depart, and the situation was so unusual, their eyes and tongues took flight. For so many years they had maintained relations of the highest courtesy and followed Carreño's maxims to the letter. But now the etiquette, the silences kept, the resentments, the solitude, the grudges that had been growing inside them without them even being aware of it, all came out, the walls of good manners came tumbling down, and things no one would have guessed were heard. Their souls were bared face-to-face, the clothing of their presumed indifference ripped to shreds. Each had unexpectedly entered the other's sphere of life and had just realized that what they felt at the bottom of their souls for each other was hatred.

"Abusive old man!"

"Crazy old woman!"

"You're the crazy one. . . . Everyone knows that!"

"Insufferably pious!"

"Maniac with matchboxes!"

"Priests' ass kisser!"

"Garbage collector!"

"Wafer swallower!"

"Cock of the walk with defenseless women!"

"Parish-house hen!"

"Good-for-nothing!"

"Old rag!"

"Stupid old man!"

"Stupid old woman!"

Aunt Clarita was stunned with emotion and shame. It was a grandiose and terrible spectacle. She never imagined that her conscientious brother and her pious sister were capable of saying what they were saying—no, yelling at each other in front of the children and the serving maids, whose ears did not miss one bit of what was happening.

Bruna wanted to join in and throw more wood on the bonfire, since the spectacle she was watching seemed more like the blaze of two jack-o'-lanterns in the small room. But she instinctively kept quiet, knowing that if she said one word, or made the slightest movement, Aunt Catalina would probably smack her with her thin, bony hands. However, she continued to approve and applaud mentally:

Good! Do it!

That's it! Bravo!

It's a tie!

Revenge!

Yes! Well put!

Good! Now you're talking.

She watched the showdown between the two powers destroying each other, two forces that meant nothing to her; in fact they poisoned and disfigured the little half-discovered world in which she lived. As long as they left Aunt Clarita alone, her aunt and her uncle could destroy each other, and the sooner the better.

Uncle Francisco ended the discussion by proclaiming, Tarzan-like, his rights as a male. It was the only time he ever did this, and it was well worth coming back from the dead to show everyone who he was. The people in the house had heard his powerful voice, seen his gestures, and been thunderstruck by his look. He pounded the table with his fist, spilling water from the jar, which slowly regained its balance, broke the last two glasses left over from the set Camelia the Tearful used during her gatherings, and left, slamming the door so hard that a faint layer of dust fell from the ceiling, through which Bruna dared to peek at Aunt Catalina, who was almost glowing.

Her aunt crossed herself as her uncle left and made various signs in the air, all of which remained in the air, supposedly conjuring up beings from hell, and ended the dispute her way as she left the dining room with her dignity intact, without saying anything or breaking anything, straight as a tablespoon, marching like a general leaving the battlefield, not defeated, but looking for reinforcements in the face of a superior enemy. Her chin trembled slightly, and she looked as if she were about to cry; but she didn't cry, not this time or ever in her life. She had no tears; she was dry inside and out. She came from the same stale lineage as her brother.

Aunt Clarita felt around under the table for her favorite niece's hand, squeezed it hard as if she were hoping to protect herself, because even though the altercation was over, there was no way of knowing what would happen next, since neither of the two contenders was ready to give way. Bruna squeezed her aunt's hand right back and understood, in her way, that the situation rested in her hands. Something should be and had to be done, something that would put an end to her uncle's lunacies and her aunt's scandalous domination. Her uncle's claim to more rooms was absurd, and if this kept up, her aunts would end up sleeping in the entranceway, on the bull vertebras that spent the night moving around, or they would be forced to beg for asylum in some convent. The matchboxes would take up all three floors of the house, then spread to the patio, cross the garden, and spill out onto the city streets just as it happened years before with Alvarito's carpet.

After the shouts, the poundings on the table, and the doors slammed on the unseen people who remained inside, the house was plunged into silence. Uncle Francisco collapsed, completely drained, on the bed where he spent his sleepless nights, tossing aside the latest package of matchboxes that he had received, tired from the long trip that he had made into the world of the living to demand his rights, and pained by his sister's lack of understanding, since he had never had one harsh or hard word with her, and he fell asleep. . . . He dreamed of a world made of matchboxes, built with the same precision that bees apply to their honeycombs. A world where candles wouldn't burn, where houses and walls would be made of tiny matchboxes, and doors and windows would be made of matchsticks, and people's hair would be made of matchsticks, and birds' throats, the clouds in the sky, the water flowing through the riverbeds, women's lips, paving stones, and aunts' lives.

Aunt Catalina, locked in her own private chapel, said the afternoon prayers and begged for heavenly protection, because she alone was incapable of fighting against her brother's tyranny and his troublesome lunacies; and she made promises to all the saints if only they would stop the invasion of matchboxes from reaching the second floor.

Bruna and Aunt Clarita went out to the patio, lost in thought, and watered the geraniums after feeding the cats, who were happy because they weren't getting a bath. Bruna sat in the patio's rocking chair and closed her eyes.

"*Una, dola, trela, canela, cabo de vela del indio panzón, piolín, piolón.* . . ."

"Eeny, meeny, miny, moe, catch a tiger by the toe. . . ."

The air was thick, as if something big were about to happen. She could almost feel it hesitating outside the big gate, and she waited for it to pull the bell rope to announce itself. If the bell didn't ring, then the event must be climbing the walls to get to the roof. Sitting on the patio, Bruna looked at her own shadow crouching beneath the rocking chair, as if it didn't dare to come out. The midday sun shone down on her head. The fish was choking on the water from the fountain. The doorbell didn't ring: the event had penetrated the house and was standing before Bruna, telling her to get out of her seat.

> *Al subir una montaña una pulga me picó,*
> *Le agarré de las narices, y se me escapó. . . .*

> I was climbing a mountain when a flea bit me,
> I grabbed it by the nose, but it got away from me. . . .

Bruna got up. She walked boldly to the kitchen. She searched in vain for a box of matches and found only some thin candles spread across the table; her uncle had passed through on his way to go lie down in his room. She held a few twigs to the hot coals that were always burning like the sacred fires in primitive times and lit a candle that she found lying nearby. Taking care that the wind didn't blow the flame out, she climbed the stairs to the second floor, then up to the third. Her knees knocked together, moving involuntarily and uncontrollably, and she was seized by physical needs, but the bathroom was miles away. . . . So her metabolic organs acted quickly, and a few drops of sweat appeared at the roots of her hair. She wanted to turn back, but the event pushed her forcefully toward the closed doors; she almost felt its hands pressing against her shoulders.

> *Pito, pito, colorito*
> *de la cera verdadera*
> *pin pon, afuera.*

Beep, beep, the colors creep
from the candle that you handle
ding, dong, run along.

She pushed the candle flame through the space between the locks. The matchboxes caught fire instantly, as if they had been waiting a long time for this, and they lit up in a range of very bright colors. The dust that covered them stepped aside courteously, allowing the candle flame to become immense. A happy crackling was heard. The event finally let go of Bruna's shoulders. An intense blue color, almost purple, climbed rapidly inside the room, twisting and turning like a roller coaster. The first rings of thick white smoke came out through the crack over the door, moving epileptically. Bruna didn't move. Fascinated by the sight, she seemed to have put down roots, until she understood that there was nothing else to do. The event, having let go of her, took possession of the house.

Everyone in the city figured that one day or another a fire would break out in the Catovils' house. It was a natural assumption for the neighbors who knew about the uncle's craziness. The people's prophecy had to be fulfilled. Bruna had no control over her actions as she brought about the future that everyone else had been waiting for. Judas must have been acting in the same way when, impelled by circumstances, he sold Jesus.

> *Tin marín de dos pingüé.*
> *Cúcara, mácara, titifué.*
> *Un inglés tiró la espada*
> *y mató al cuarenta y tres. . . .*

> One, two, buckle my shoe
> Three, four, open the door.
> An Englishman drew his sword
> and then he killed all forty-four.

The fire-starter ran home, feeling as if the event were following her and wanted to make her go back so it could lock her in the rooms where the matchboxes had been turned to ashes. When she got there, without meaning to she kicked Panchita, who went flying right into a metal umbrella stand. A deafening noise was heard. Bruna thought she was lost, and deep inside herself she felt relieved, because it was crazy to spend your whole life running, turning your feet into scissors that would cut you off from everything, checking under the bed before getting in to sleep, looking into the bottom of a glass to see if anyone was submerged in the water you were about to drink, cautiously opening the pages of a book out of fear that someone would be hiding among the letters, constantly turning your head to make sure that no one was following you, feeling around in the darkness with your fingers to find out if you were really alone or accompanied by someone who would never leave you. . . .

Panchita was a dirty old cloth coffee filter with a hole in the bottom. She was her sister's favorite doll, which she slept with and played with all day. . . . She was dressed in the clothes of real dolls, who were dying with jealousy of the old coffee filter. Panchita was constantly getting the very essence of motherly love on her tiny mouth, which Bruna's sister gave warm, noisy kisses.

"Bedtime!"

"I'm not going!"

"Why not?"

"Because Panchita's not tired."

"You're going to school next year."

"No, no, and no. Panchita doesn't want to learn how to read!"

Two hours later the firemen's alarm sounded. The church bells coughed as their clappers tasted the first tendrils of smoke. People shouted:

"Fire, fire!"

And everyone knew where it was. The city's garbagemen were running around in despair because their profitable business was finished. The imps took off their hats to catch the flying sparks. The devils applauded with their wings and made cabalistic signs with their tails. Old women went looking for the holy palms that were nailed behind the doors to keep fires from coming in. The sparks wedded with the air, producing tiny black offspring that flew off in all directions. The fire, locked up for so long inside the matchboxes, proclaimed its independence and, singing the first songs of liberty, climbed the first step toward heaven.

"Fire, fire!"

"It's got to be the Catovils' house. . . ."

"Fire! The whole city's burning!"

Pale and trembling beneath the weight of the guilt on her miserable shoulders, Bruna dug her fingernails into her palms until she drew blood. Her mother happened to pass by, and on a sudden, desperate impulse Bruna told her the truth:

"I did it, mamá, I started the fire. Poor Aunt Clarita was . . ."

But the truth came out of her mouth so frightened and misdirected that it seemed like a made-up story. The story made fun of the truth, and the truth escaped between her words. She was told to be quiet: the name "Catovil" was being spoken too much in the city. Seeing how pale she was, they gave her a teaspoon of Scott's Emulsion and sent her to bed.

What followed was a nightmarish and unforgettable night in the family's saga, with everyone running in and out and the two aunts screaming from the safety of Bruna's house, having acquired the unfamiliar prestige of being the rightful owners of the fire, while Uncle Francisco gave the firemen directions.

A fever consumed Bruna, making her fly through the diffuse worlds of unconsciousness; the only thing that she remembered afterward was Aunt Catalina screaming to save Aunt Clarita from the fire, and the efforts of her family, led by her mother, struggling to insert a thermometer in her rectum to take her temperature.

The fever lasted for three days, with characteristic nightmares in which she saw gigantic yellow shapes coming out of her own skin that were so big that, even turning her head, she couldn't take in their full size, although she could somehow sense their volume. These shapes bumped into each other, got lost, and flew away. She felt them inside her body and was crushed beneath their great weight.

In the chaotic world of her nightmares the word "fire" reached her from the distant conversations that reached her ears without her being able to make out their meaning. For three days she wandered in the hazy world of alcohol rubs and dabs of methylene blue dye that they applied to the inside of her throat with cotton. When she rose from the bed, the terrible event had lost its sheen. The third floor and the gossip had disappeared. The second floor was still warm. And Bruna was paler and much, much thinner.

20

Bruna remembered the family house and the details of her child-hood while a sadness gnawed away at her heart like a mouse trapped inside her looking for way out, knowing that unfortunately one lives only once and that a beautiful, full life, as deep as the limitless sea, is barely an atom in the eternity of time.

You live for forty, seventy, eighty years—few people live longer—consciously choosing to live a long, full life, not one wasted by too many absurd preoccupations, or going nowhere because you were born at the wrong time. . . . Life is a drop of time in a place called the world in which we see only the thousandth part of all things.

"I'd like to see the Taj Mahal!"

"And me, the pyramids of Egypt. . . ."

"I'd like to visit the city of Alexandria."

"And I'd like to visit a ziggurat."

Life goes by without feeling all the sensations one could feel:

"What would it feel like to jump out of a plane with a para-chute?"

"What would it feel like to win the lottery and be able to run your life the way you wanted to?"

"Or if you met face-to-face with a mutant?"

"Or went on a space voyage?"

Life goes by without knowing all the people who contain so many other infinite universes:

"How do the Soviets live?"

"How do the Eskimos live?"

"How do the Australians live?"

Life goes by without feeling all of the few ecstasies that fill in the gaps in the hours, or all the sadness or happiness that gives existence its color and taste.

The world, far from getting smaller owing to the advances of science and the wonders of crossing tremendous distances in a few fractions of a second, is growing, because the possibilities are growing, too rapidly to be able to cover the fullness of what is called "having lived," to be able to leave behind, without pain or remorse, the marvelous mechanism of the body, converted into the macabre feast of worms.

"We're over thirty, so we'll never get to go to the moon. . . ."

"Or be able to hibernate. . . ."

"And what's worse, no more living in the land of laziness. . . ."

Bruna had reached the moment when she had to grab on, with her hands, fingernails, and teeth, and hold on to the belief in the resurrection of the flesh in order for her life to have direction and for her good deeds to make a minimum of sense; the belief in which love and goodness lie down together, in which all things and beings in the universe are equal. If no one or nothing could convince her, then she would have to convince herself:

"I hope there's another life. . . . I hope there's another life. . . . I hope there's another life. . . ."

The years we spend living on the earth, even with all of our senses wide open and aware of things, are still not enough for everybody; there's a minority who feel cheated and who will always carry the infinite sadness of nonconformity. For the majority it's fine that life is the way it is; why should nearsighted people ask for more?

"The world is full of problems? I didn't know that."

Why should the great mass of people want to live longer when they spend their lives crouched on their pain and doing nothing but groaning?

"What do I care about the war in Vietnam if I've got my own problems?"

Why should the spiritually sick want to live longer when they can try to heal themselves with massive doses of egotism?

"My son got married and abandoned me."

"My stomach hurts. I'm so sick!"

"Let them protest, I don't have time."

Life is fine just the way it is for people who have grown accustomed to cloaking their eyes with the cobwebs of their own shadows. For those who accept suffering like a tortoise accepts its shell, and who can't crawl out of or shake off their pain, who carry all their little disappointments like a snail shell on their backs, groaning, startling the world with their complaints, denying the sun when it comes out because all they can see are their own feet, ignorant of spring because they spend their lives stuck in the longest of winters, not knowing about flowers because they can't distinguish colors, without realizing that children are being born and that with each birth one can fool oneself into thinking that maybe they're being reborn . . . unable to greet a friend because they never take their hands out of their pockets, not knowing that there are sick people who can be cured with a smile, absences that stop being so with a letter, and insults that can be forgiven because a place has been found to put them: oblivion.

Bruna thought that life was the most marvelous adventure, as only the mind of a well-meaning God could conceive it, yet she also rebelled because for her it was a sliver of wood, a speck of dust, even though it was an offering of inconceivable generosity on the part of the giver. . . .

Only a few days were left before they were going to demolish the old family house. They were going to tear down the walls that sheltered so many orphaned lives and so many generations. They were going to tear out the doors and windows by the roots in the same way that they tore María Illacatu's children away from her side.

They were going to destroy the fountain with the graceful "pisstatue" that replaced the horrible stone fish. They were going to fell the generous cherry tree that never got tired of giving away its fruit and that witnessed the treasure chest getting up and walking away one night. They were going to destroy the lemon trees in whose shadows Mama Chana mended her baubles and the children's socks. They were going to be amazed at the rim of the well when they discovered that it was dark and dry. . . .

The house's new owners were Mama Chana's descendants. They had taken a tour from the entranceway to the orchard, appraising everything they saw:

"The house is in bad shape, but the property . . ."

Things had taken a painful turn after the death of Uncle Francisco. The new owners had no idea of the true value of money or how to use it.

"We're going to put up a building with forty-two apartments."

Bruna had to make her living tied to a secretary's desk for eleven months out of the year in order to live one month of full, absolute life. During that month she broke the routines that turned her into a screw in an absurd machine and breathed in happiness, far away from stupid bosses whom she had to obey. But in spite of this and everything else, life was beautiful; she would never get tired of repeating it. She wanted to live again, even though the world would always be what it was, at the expense of all else, even if she were reborn trapped in a wheelchair, sick, an invalid, but herself, herself alone, with her wealth of unending love and her undiminished power to fall in love with a single thing: life.

On the wall that they were tearing down, which used to be part of Aunt Catalina's room, was a photo of Uncle Francisco. It was a bad photo, and it was eaten away by moisture. You couldn't even touch it with the tip of your finger or it would crumble to dust. It was like the reflection in the pond: if the water moved, the image disappeared in its depths. The new owners brought in a professional photographer to make an enlargement of the master of the house.

"Be careful, be very careful. It has to come out right. This is a photo of our grandfather!"

They didn't know the family stories, because Mama Chana had died, taking with her the secret that it would have hurt them to know, and even though they had their doubts about their origins, they didn't want to dig too deeply into them out of fear that people would call them nouveau riche.

They removed the portrait of the Indian grandmother, taking it down with all due care, since their new social position was riding on it. But in spite of everything, they lived in constant suspense, without a past, their foundations built on sand, which would make the new building shudder at the first questions from curious friends:

"How distinguished, how elegant! Who is this señora?"

"She's our grandmother."

"But, wasn't your grandmother Señora Josefa?"

"Then, this is her mother."

"So . . . this is Señora Encarnita?"

"Yes, yes . . . that's her."

"But she doesn't look anything like her. . . ."

They were lost in the byways of the family name and preferred living in the shadows, maybe even in poverty, before admitting that Mama Chana was the serving maid in a house that had come down in the world. And Mama Chana, maid, embroiderer, half witch, with no more social holdings than the kitchen and the shadow of the old lemon trees, now gave them a position of privilege. And in denying who she was, they really debased themselves.

"La Chanita? She was our housekeeper."

"Ah! Now I understand."

The great lady in the portrait turned into the ancestor of an invented history that kept changing according to the circumstances of the future generations, until the painting got lost in the shadows of a museum under the title "The Unknown Woman." That's when the pieces of María Illacatu's soul that had remained suspended from the tips of the stars joined one by one and became a reality again.

135

21

In the awful photo that they finally made of him, the new family's new grandfather was leaning on a walking stick with a shiny handle. He had a slightly sly smile that he never had in life because he was really a sad, dreary, lonely man. The worm of loneliness laid its larvae in his bones. He couldn't shake off the hidden sadness bequeathed to him by his Indian grandmother. He walled himself in behind the matchboxes because the world, which for him was the sleeping city, scared him.

He carried the stigma of solitude, which is the saddest stigma. The women in the family put up with him better than the men did. As if solitude were the hooded cloak of a penitent sinner, the women knew how to adjust the pleats of the cloak to fit his body better, so they could walk through life with more elegance, less disdain, and less humiliation. The men wasted away under his weight, living condemned lives and seeking refuge in the world of the absurd. They married madness and from there gave birth to thousands of aberrations, which took on life and flesh in future generations that would eventually be tossed from the five floors of the house; or they would follow in the footsteps of the wandering Jew, carrying the craziest delusions around as baggage; the ones who covered their heads with wide-brimmed hats and tore out their eyes trying to look backward were the same ones whose bodies shrank, transforming them into the imps who walked along the roof tiles, throwing stones at pregnant women and children who told lies.

Uncle Francisco took refuge in insanity, and that insanity made him a more pious man, unable to struggle with a world in which no one offered him any love. Reality was stifling, and sensitivity was discouraged and denigrated. The *soroche* had wrapped him in its vapors since the day that his aunt left the convent to take care of him, and since he never took the pills, there was nothing he could do about it.

The era in which he lived was the sleeping city's darkest and most impersonal era. The mountains confined the city to the most isolated corner of all geography. The people who lived there managed to convince themselves that they were alone on the planet and dedicated themselves to living on gossip and the past. They had no other ambition but to increase the number of flowering buds on the family trees that gave them birth. And thousands of bastards toiled, heroically searching for and trying to stretch a triangular heraldic symbol to cover their naked cradles, and grew up to be insecure cowards with someone else's guilt complex.

Those who were born with other ambitions, like poets, turned out badly, climbing a distant Parnassus to carry off a nymph or a maiden—never a flesh-and-blood woman—to put in the lines of their brittle, crumbly verses. Real women weighed too much, whereas nymphs could be made to walk across their writing desks, between the inkwells and paperweights, and even jump into the air so they wouldn't dirty their golden sandals. They invented a new sex for the women who walked barefoot through the stone streets, suffering in the flesh and feeling in their deepest souls the clash of the two cultures that ensnared them, and the pain of carrying in their own wombs a third culture that, as it gestated, was nourished by two bloodlines that hated each other. . . .

The poor women didn't know which way to direct or to push the new generation so that they would be born under a roof that could shelter them and yet also within the framework that recognized and legitimated property ownership. The culture that was born had no sense of what it should love and what it should hate. It liked the splendor and supremacy of the one part, but when they approached, they were rejected because of the color of their skin. They went over to the other side, the side of misery, but had to abandon it in order to survive, and also because the color of their skin didn't fit in well with that side, either. The cultures didn't unite, or mix, or understand each other.

They lived at a time when there were only two daily occupations: prayer and gossip. Doors and minds were closed, and initiatives were locked in cages.

Liberty was just a word.

A culture had been born and imposed, filling the marrow of their bones, while their own was denigrated.

Liberty was just a word.

God was hidden behind all the solid gold objects in the churches because he had stopped speaking to them, and they tried to smother the Gospel's simplicity under ghastly wigs made of human hair and robes embroidered with fine jewels, because a sense of justice was beyond their abilities. They worshiped a God who was full of blood and bruises because religion came to them through violence.

Liberty was just a word.

They lived for the pleasure of endless torchlight processions of penitent sinners who left their footsteps on the sharp rocks, dampening them with their blood, staggering under the weight of crosses that blistered and scraped their skin down to the raw flesh. They applauded the ones who wore crowns of genuine thorns around their heads that pierced their temples without penetrating their minds. They smiled complacently at the humbling of the flesh as someone whipped himself with a lead-tipped cat-o'-nine-tails. And as the lead left its marks in the flesh, a smile would appear on a penitent's lips when he saw in the crowd, awed by the grim and bloody spectacle, the face of some neighbor or a pair of eyes full of tears of remorse and repentance.

"Here come the penitents!"

"Look at the blood flow!"

"How the bells ring!"

"It feels like a holiday. . . ."

They glutted themselves with solemn, high Masses where the old folks beat their breasts heavily and the young ones sent coded messages to each other with the tips of their eyelashes.

"... *qui tollis peccata mundi* ..."

"I want to marry you. . . ."

They increased the impulsive stock of illegitimate children, because although they all wished to spend their evenings at the house of the Bello Animal, few dared to frequent it.

"Don Martín came home at two in the morning. . . ."

"He must have been with the plump women. . . ."

"The shameful man . . . and during Lent!"

They cured themselves with bloodlettings. They lived next door to prisons where the mentally ill were tortured because everyone believed that they had made pacts with the Devil. They heard the clandestine footsteps of wayward monks, creeping toward scandal like moles. They took part, thrilling in the idiotic revolutions of the liberals and conservatives. They bowed reverently before the flashy tinsel of the military men who figured in the political scene, behaving like the soldiers in an operetta, multiplying and decorating themselves with intrigues manipulated by women and megalomaniacs. They unflinchingly and uncaringly contemplated the total destruction of womankind, which they foresaw in the armies of poor *guarichas* who infected the streets and towns with pain and disgrace.

"Ay, my country! . . ."

"If you love it, change it. Erase all the boundaries."

"Yes, life is change. . . ."

22

To her nieces and nephews, Aunt Catalina—*caca de gallina*—was the biggest known enemy of the world, flesh and the Devil. She was the impersonal personified, the inhuman in human form. She was a scarecrow in the middle of a wasteland. The right shoe for someone with a crippled left leg. An oil lamp in the bright sun and all the children's bogeyman.

"Why was Aunt Catalina born?"

"To torture us our whole lives. . . ."

"When will Aunt Catalina—*caca de gallina*—die?"

"Never, never. . . ."

Her craziness wasn't as obvious as her brother's, it was just more organized: you could see him shrink himself down to fit inside a matchbox, where he kept quiet and didn't bother anybody. With her, you didn't see her so much as feel her presence from the effect she had on things, people, and animals: the geraniums on the patio went pale or closed up whenever she passed by. The children's faces and hands would stiffen, and Aunt Clarita's Angora cats would start twitching when they saw her.

"Aunt Catalina is very pious."

"Come on! She's an old crackpot."

"Aunt Catalina is a saint."

"That's a lie, she's a crazy old woman!"

"Don't say such things! Go wash your mouth out with soap!"

Her parents died when she was a child, and they dressed her in black, and ever since then she remained dressed in black for the never-ending deaths in the family that came one after the other. So the color entered her body, and she was never seen dressed in anything other than black.

"I have never, *never* worn garish colors in my life, like those loose women do!"

"Aunt Clarita isn't a loose woman, and she wears colorful clothing."

"She does whatever she wants, with no respect for the memory of the dead."

Her strange shape loomed over every corner of the house like a Chinese shadow puppet. Her thoughts were black. Her pupils were black and had the peculiar ability to penetrate people's thoughts and tear them to shreds. All of her clothes were black, from her socks to her handkerchiefs. She received all of Death's hand-me-downs once they had gone out of style.

Even though Aunt Catalina had been born in the sleeping city, she always told everyone that she was a citizen of the "valley of tears." This citizenship was authenticated by a paper that she carried that was signed by all the sacristans in the world. She felt that she had to atone for having been born and, faithful to her destiny, dedicated herself to purging herself and everyone else of their shortcomings, going up to heaven and down to hell every day and wishing for a processional chair just like the pope's, only built to her measurements, which had the power to fly like a witch's broomstick so that she could inspect what the people of the city were doing and stick her wrinkled nose into everyone's business, for the common good. If Aunt Catalina had lived a few years later, she wouldn't have stopped until she got the job of public entertainment censor.

The lengthy prayers that lost their way on a long, winding path to nowhere still echoed in one's ears:

"*Ora pro nobisss. Miserere nobisss. . . .*"

The holy water that she submerged herself in like a duck in a pond, and the penitential acts that took off pieces of her skin, were her daily bread. She lived and died so that morality would take root in the world, dedicating herself to her mission with an eagerness of one possessed that flowed in her blood, weighed down her hands, and blinded her eyes.

Aunt Catalina stood out, tall and thin. She had twilight in her ears, and her skin was yellow from the endless fasting and other deprivations that she underwent. She drew her hair tightly back, making it look as if a hurricane were blowing in her face. The complicated hair clasp at the back of her neck was made of a mixture of the following: gum arabic, a variety of old socks, and the swarm of busy bees that were Mama Chana's fingers. The hair clasp had three parts, arranged from largest to smallest, which were made in the name of the Father, and of the Son, and of the Holy Spirit.

She loved the sad, the gloomy, and the somber. She was the constant widow at vespers, the grave digger's mother, the embalmer of children who weren't even dead yet. Everything she touched took on a breath of the otherworldly that got under the skin of anyone who was near her, making them shiver.

She was always chasing her nephews and hitting them on the head with her large rosary.

"*Guambras peccata mundi!* Children of the Devil!"

She assured them that the Devil was watching them from inside the mouth of the fish that she herself had put there, or among the stones of the pillars that held up the second floor, and swore that she had seen Satan himself come near the children's ears, in the shape of a mosquito, to induce them to do nasty things.

"With my own eyes that will someday be dust and ashes I saw the Evil One secretly telling you that. . . ."

The boys' mouths dropped open, and doubt flew into their open mouths. They didn't understand the expression "nasty things," but they imagined a subhuman world, some kind of strange animal that was growing inside one of the locked rooms, something that they couldn't quite understand in the hushed conversations, a bit of blushing they managed to glimpse on the masks the adults wore and that, after all, attracted them because of its mystery and because their aunt made it quite clear that it repulsed her.

Getting hit on the head hurt so much because the blows wounded them deep inside, in the realm of the untouchable, where their images of themselves were being born, the minds and bodies of tomorrow.

The blows filled Bruna with a blind rage that started deep within, squirmed around, and finally exploded from her in curses that escaped through her teeth. After hitting them with the rosary, their aunt relented and handed out candies that tasted of wax and tears and left their tongues and palates all pinched and shriveled.

"Have a candy, so you'll be a good boy! Let's see, hold out your hand! It's as dirty as your conscience! Go wash it in the fountain!"

"My conscience?"

"Idiot, you wash that in the holy sacrament of penitence!"

Aunt Catalina had a mania for indulgences. She had the second floor all to herself, except for Aunt Clarita's bedroom. The whole floor was a kind of office of liturgical information, where you could find any detail about the life of any saint and all of the information published to date about indulgences that had reached the city. Above the second floor was the leftover debris from the fire. When Aunt Catalina was there, the floor swayed and suddenly rose toward the clouds, took a turn around the kingdom of heaven, and fell back into place, without the aunt who was inside it noticing anything.

The large drawing room, where the Indian grandmother was surrounded by discretion and silence, the big rooms, little rooms, and anterooms that dated from a period of wealth long past, and where sometimes Aunt Camelia the Tearful came to finish one of her gatherings after it had been interrupted by the roosters crowing, had all been converted into the central offices where Aunt Catalina ran the big business of her life and her salvation.

"What does it serve to win the whole world, if in the end I lose my soul? . . ."

Aunt Catalina created an unbridgeable gap between heaven and the earth, filled with thousand-year-old monsters with enormous open jaws whose teeth were made of the tiny heads of unborn children. The aunt had to walk through this terrible place. She had to carry it with her, dragging it by the tongue with her own body. She had to crush it, bruise it, shake it among the stars, the thunder and lightning, to strip it of its hateful flesh. She covered the eyes of her body so that she wouldn't be tempted to look at a sunset or the daisies growing on the hillsides. Her body was no more than the hide; she had made the organs disappear on a forced march toward eternity.

"Why was I born?"

"To save myself."

"Because I have to die."

"It's inevitable. . . ."

Aunt Catalina won more than one million indulgences in a single day. It took her five seconds to say:

"Sacred heart of Jesus, I trust in you."

This little outburst left her with a net gain of three hundred days of indulgence. She said the same outburst twelve times in one minute. Since she was afraid of appearing to profit from such an easy business, but mostly to make the calculations easier, she lowered her rate to ten outbursts per minute: ten times three hundred equals three thousand indulgences per minute. Three thousand times sixty equals one hundred eighty thousand indulgences per hour. She spent almost the whole day at this mathematical practice, sometimes standing at the summit of the roof, emulating Joshua and successfully stopping the sun in its tracks and creating, just for her, twenty-five- and even thirty-hour days.

She went to three Masses a day in summer and two a day in winter. When it rained in the city, the water didn't run through the streets but stayed between the stones, sleeping in a prolonged muddy dream, and Aunt Catalina had to walk along, jumping from rock to rock, supported by the tip of her umbrella. Sometimes she got lost on her way to church and had to go out of her way, which put her in a rotten mood. She would finish her prayers shivering, with a moist vapor rising from her clothes. Her shadow stayed under the knee rest in church, until one day the sun came out, and she went and got it and brought it back to the house. Every time she thought about the vast amount of indulgences she had accumulated, she would kneel down and kiss the ground so that vanity would not make her vain. But every time she knelt and kissed the ground she got pains in her lower abdomen, which put her in a rotten mood again. She visited hundreds of churches and made pilgrimages to the innumerable hermitages that were seated on the folds of the mountain's lower slopes, for which she was rewarded with several thousand more indulgences, which weren't always directly related, or practical, but which nevertheless left her with a safe profit margin.

The numbers were too much for her. Her head, already considerably weakened by so much fasting, got more and more hollowed out. It seemed to be filled with millions of white and black butterflies that flew out of her mouth in long, orderly rows whenever she prayed.

Every day Aunt Catalina made herself more incapable of doing anything that wasn't related to indulgences. She was growing more bitter and tolerating less from the children: she hated their laughter, because it felt like fine crystal being broken and crushed underfoot; their noise bothered her, and their pranks gave her mind a severe rash; their movements and even the way they grew, so healthy and strong, annoyed her.

"Don't shout. Don't laugh like that. Don't run. What are you hiding in your hand? Why is your door shut?"

Sometimes she imagined that the children were enormous colored balloons that could burst at any moment. She hated how they gobbled up the fruits from the orchard and the way they made candy on Thursday afternoons.

"Gluttony is also a sin."

She couldn't stand the innocence with which they asked such terrible questions, and especially the curiosity they showed watching the cats mating, which made her feel as if she were living in Sodom and Gomorrah.

"Chana! The cats! Throw boiling water on them for being impure!"

Her many friends, who were also in the habit of taking off for the stars, holding on to bats' claws on moonlit nights, and coming back more bitter than ever the next morning, counseled her to patiently carry the cross that had been imposed on her, and they gave her rules and standards so that she would not be overcome by wrath and in that way fall from the state of grace that was the essential condition for her dedicating herself to the practice of indulgences. She made unspeakable efforts, and when she lost her patience, which she carried around in the bags under her eyes, she justified her anger as "holy wrath," because it resembled the wrath of Moses when he came down from Mount Sinai and saw what he saw. . . .

As time went by and the great quantity of indulgences accumulated, she had to get an assistant. She couldn't find a single woman who was able to do it—which was what she wanted—because all the women in the sleeping city were very busy themselves. They were embroidering chrysanthemums and forget-me-nots on large linen sheets to give to their husbands or boyfriends on their birthdays. It had become the fashion to give embroidered shrouds to your loved ones. . . . In addition, the women spent so much time on funereal rites that they had forgotten what little arithmetic they had managed to learn. Aunt Catalina, much to her displeasure, had no choice but to hire a young man who was skilled at bookkeeping to help her keep track of the business of her salvation.

"Why don't you like the young man?"

"That's it exactly. Because he's young and I have to be alone all day with him. . . ."

"But Catalina! At your age!"

"Not on my account! God preserve me! But the Devil is everywhere."

"Yes . . . you're right. Even between saints, a wall of mortar and stone."

She didn't allow any men around her because she considered them to be more lustful, more understanding of, and more in harmony with the Devil than women, who because of their superior constitutions—she said—circled around a few more times before falling into temptation, and while they were circling, they still knew how to be gracious. . . .

It was hard for her to admit the existence of women who had to live alone, abandoned by the lustfulness of men, and she felt that a family needed the support of a masculine presence, even if that presence were only the appearance of such, as in the case of her crazy brother.

"And what are we going to do now, the two of us alone, completely alone, without a man in the house?"

"The house is safe."

"I'm not talking about that."

She had never stopped to think that, at a certain age, a woman could lose her sexuality; she felt that women were always in danger of taking a false step, because:

"The Devil is everywhere. . . . And Clara and I are alone. I don't even want to think about it."

And that was how she came up with the brilliant idea of offering the employee whom she had contracted double his salary if, during office hours, he would present himself before her dressed as a woman.

"Señora!"

"Señorita, señorita! And say it with respect!"

"Señorita, I wouldn't do it for a hundred sucres!"

The young man turned red at the proposition and threatened to walk out and leave her in charge of the numbers. So they managed, after many detours and much give-and-take, to get the young man to dress during work hours in a blue-black apron that covered his arms and reached down to his ankles. The young man let himself be convinced and started to work. Aunt Clarita made the apron, and when the nieces and nephews saw him, they couldn't contain their laughter.

"Why are you wearing that apron?"

"Because your blasted—uh, blessed aunt ordered me to."

"And why are you turning red, hmm?"

"Because I feel like it."

When the young man realized whom he was dealing with, he started doing his job in a way that made the aunt happy, even though mathematically his accounting left much to be desired. But the work was certainly up-to-date. The aunt smiled for the first time in her life. She had in her favor the incredible sum of 425,822 centuries of indulgences!

With such a number—she said—there wasn't a human or divine power that could even make her pass through the gates of purgatory. She paid a very high price, and her efforts had bought her a place in the chorus of the "Eleven Thousand Virgins."

"*Now* the gates of hell are shut for me! I'll be the newest member of that chorus because that's where I want them to put me."

"But Aunt, your guardian angel won't be able to stand next to you there."

"Maybe my angel's a female angel. . . ."

She pictured herself in this chorus. Only then would she stop wearing black; she would spend eternity in the white dress she wore at her first communion, with a crown of white lilies on her head.

When the euphoria passed, Aunt Catalina started to distrust the young secretary's accounting and the method he had used for reducing the insignificant seconds into solid centuries, and she demanded that he present her with a most detailed report.

"I want to be able to see all the numbers at once on a single piece of paper. Understand?"

The poor young man, his head already spinning from all the numbers, started to fidget, and seeing that all was lost, he offered his resignation. Aunt Catalina jumped.

"You can't just leave me like that! I'll pay you whatever you want!"

The resignation was not accepted in view of the work that remained to be done. So, for everyone's peace of mind, someone suggested that the aunt get an adding machine, and she ordered a machine from the far-off country where they made so many machines that they even had machines to make machines.

Months later an enormous crate arrived that contained the adding machine. The whole family got together to look at it and touch it. People rushed into the streets when they heard the rumor that the Catovils had a machine that made indulgences.

"Let's go see the sacred machine!"

"Don't say stupid things, there aren't any sacred machines!"

"But this one makes indulgences, and it's imported!"

Many visitors came to the house, and Aunt Catalina spent the happiest days of her life feeling as if she were standing on top of a mountain made of shares of holy stock.

The young accountant took charge of the marvelous piece of equipment and learned how to work it in a flash. He recovered from the insults to his virility, and only then did he dare to reclaim his rights. He gave the blue-black apron a symbolic kick in the behind and sent it flying under a bookcase filled with pious books, where it remained for many years, hidden like the sheep's clothing thrown off by a fierce wolf. He made sure that the creases of his pants were straight and well ironed, and he bought a tie with muted colors whose knot he adjusted every time someone came into the office. Little by little he began to look at Bruna for longer periods of time, and she in turn found him likable and started to visit the old family house more diligently than ever, plundering Aunt Clarita's dressing table, looking for the bottle of 4711 cologne that her aunt put on her hands and hair. Then she would go visit her other aunt's pious offices.

During the hours that the young man was in the house the only sound that could be heard was the *cric-clac* of the adding machine's lever, and sometimes the silence was interrupted by Bruna's laughter, which purified the air and brought out the colors of the potted geraniums in the courtyard. The fish shut its big, ugly mouth, the water fell more quietly, and major financial activity took place in Aunt Catalina's big rooms, where more numbers were handled than in the stock exchange on Wall Street.

"How does this machine work, hmm?"

"Like this. It's very easy. Do you want to try it?"

"All right. . . . Is this okay? Like this?"

Secure that the salvation of her soul was a done deal, since the practice that the aunt had given herself over to came with more guarantees than the feat of saying the Lord's Prayer in the exact time it took to watch a shooting star fall from the sky—as their unfortunate grandmother had done (the one who wrote the names of Adam and Eve with the blood from her nose before she died)—the aunt thought that, to avoid being idle, she could help the next person. Since she was interested in neither the present nor the earthly, since the things that came in contact with her hands left them covered with mold, she dedicated herself with true frenzy to getting souls out of purgatory so that those souls whose sentences had been reduced could accompany her on her triumphal entrance into the kingdom of heaven.

In one year she got out thirty-five million souls, many of whom—she believed—must have been black from so much soot. But even so, she assumed that she had gotten them out and that those souls were wandering around the atmosphere, waiting for her to die so that they could ascend to heaven together.

When she realized how easy it was to get souls out of purgatory she swore by all the saints, including herself, that she wouldn't rest until she had completely emptied out all of purgatory. . . .

"I will do it. As God is my witness, I will do it."

23

The few times that the Catovil family managed to get together it was usually for the purpose of celebrating one of the aunts' or the uncle's birthdays. Year after year during these get-togethers the family discussed the same topic, which was the insistence that their ancestors were models of virtue and that kids today weren't the way kids used to be. Little by little problems surfaced and the nieces and nephews joined the tournament of discussion topics:

"Gabriel shat out a tapeworm this big! Alive and wiggling!"

"Didn't I tell you that God would cure you with a dose of calomel?"

"Martita is constipated. . . ."

"We have to give her a slice of onion as a suppository."

Aunt Catalina wanted one of her many nephews to study to become an expert accountant so that he could help her with the business of indulgences and so she wouldn't need to count on strangers from outside the family who would go around telling everyone about their most intimate lives, which could arouse envy and malicious comments among the people of the city whose lives were given over to other, less important business. In addition, these strangers had to be with her all day, a contact that was nearly promiscuous and didn't suit her at all.

"I need a nephew of my own blood to replace this young man."

"How about Pedrito?"

"No, he's still a snot-nosed little kid."

"Then . . ."

Her censor's instincts told her that something was wrong, and she crossed herself about her suspicion. She imagined a romance with fatal consequences between the young secretary and her oldest niece, which in reality didn't go beyond innocent flirting between a girl who was becoming a woman and trying to escape from *soroche* and a guy who had taken off the belittling apron and bought a tie and who was so happy about it that he went so far as to glue decals of butterflies to the weekly reports he submitted to the aunt.

"I demand an explanation of this!"

"It's a decal. . . ."

"I-know-that!"

"I figured that—"

"What a shameless man. You have no respect for God or the saints!"

"I thought that—"

"Prepare me another report im-me-di-ate-ly!"

She started to get worried. Her catlike sense of smell, perfected and maintained by the constant daily sacrifice of smelling other people's deeds in order to catalog the people as good or evil, put her on the trail of a hunting expedition that was going on in her own house, whose catch was pursued by base desires.

"I don't like it, I don't like it that Bruna comes around here so much. . . ."

"Why?"

"Because of the young man. You understand?"

"No, I don't understand. Have you seen anything?"

"An ounce of prevention . . ."

Then Aunt Clarita realized the way things were going, and it didn't seem bad; the canaries were singing in their cages and staying in tune, the parakeets in the garden, for the first time in zoological history, were thinking about what they were saying as they screeched the names of the two young people: Brunaaa! Manueeel! And the cats' fur was shinier than ever; the cats, ashamed of their laziness, thought about maybe chasing some mice the way the rest of the cats in the world did. And in the bottom of the well, it seemed as if the eye of the Devil had been blinded forever and no longer looked into the tortuous depths of people's souls, where nobody could look themselves without being in danger of becoming diabolical.

"Bruna is growing up, we have to keep an eye on her."

"Why?"

"You're always on the moon. Also, we have to make her a school jacket that fits her better."

"What for?"

"What do you think it's for?"

"But the poor girl doesn't have anything yet. . . ."

"You, and her mother, might as well be roaming around Bethlehem with the shepherds."

Between her aunts' watchful looks and the lemon tree buds that were just starting to open, Bruna felt something like love. One afternoon when Aunt Clarita stayed in bed with a chill and Aunt Catalina had gone on a pilgrimage to assure a positive credit balance in an indulgence account that was a bit short, Bruna and the young secretary escaped to the orchard; and as if they had planned it beforehand, they gave each other a kiss. Bruna drew previously unknown power from the feeling, and, clinging to the young man's hand, she leaned over the mouth of the well, looked at the bottom, and saw the bright, still water and nothing else.

"Let's go look down the well!"

"Let's go!"

"Give me your hand! Look! There's nothing there, nothing!"

Afterward she suddenly understood the value of the kiss. There was something inexplicably beautiful about it. It could transport her to faraway places, restless and undecided places. She needed a favorable setting like the long row of lemon trees and the discretion of the garden, where the only watchers were the cabbages and artichokes that could keep a secret under their thousands of leaves. Bruna's kiss was a step toward the obscure world of others, which

153

could be entered without violence, without fear of breaking anything, because she was sure to find light in the most hard-to-reach
places. It was an act of solidarity with the young man, and of justice, because he worked under the command of a dreadful boss, her
aunt, and because he had put on an apron, and because he was
being drained by the stupid and oppressive job of enclosing in the
world of numbers acts so pointless that they had the weight of a
feather, but which were nevertheless capable of deciding eternal salvation or condemnation.

Once she had tasted her first kiss, Bruna remembered there was
another young man who lived next door to her house with whom
she exchanged long looks that carried words back and forth with
them, and that she liked him more than the young secretary because
he had never put on an apron and because he had the power to
make Bruna's blood flow to her cheeks and to change the rhythm of
her movements with an inexplicable happiness. She shoved the
young secretary aside; he stood there, amazed, thinking that the
Catovil family's craziness was an absolute fact and not just gossip,
the people of the sleeping city merely exercising their tongues.

"Hey, Bruna! What's going on? Come back here!"

It was that time of day when the air stops at the corners just like
a policeman, when Bruna and the other young man happened—or
planned it so that they happened—to come in and out of their
respective houses. Bruna came running like a cyclone from the
orchard, and when the young man arrived, almost without stopping
she planted a kiss right in the middle of his mouth. The afternoon
drew its shadows under the closed windows. The shadows climbed
up the faces of the houses, pushing the sun away, and the sun slid
under the roots of the mountain. The closed doors opened . . . and
love was born.

Bruna became a woman overnight. She suddenly understood
what the kiss meant, in all its shades, and its sliding scale of power
for which people walked, rose, fell, flew. . . .

She flew into her house like a whirlwind, kissed her little brothers one by one on their heads, which smelled of lime and chamomile, and where the nighttime angels left a line down the middle of their heads with the tips of their wings as they pulled the hair away from their eyes so that they could see what they were dreaming better. . . .

Bruna kept giving everybody kisses. It was a lie that the mouth was made for eating or laughing. The mouth was made for kissing.

24

Bruna's parents were those extraordinary characters who came from the countryside after the death of the thousand Indians who worked their land. Even though they were married cousins, their children were physically normal, inheriting from their grandparents a form of nonconformity that, if examined closely, turned out to be a natural immunity against the ills of *soroche.*

Bruna's parents became uncomfortable when they heard the aunt saying that she wanted one of their children to become an expert accountant. María the Twenty-third and her husband wanted their children to be professionals, and they didn't like the idea of Aunt Catalina taking charge of any of them, even though she had promised to pay for their education, which would be in a country on the other side of the ocean.

"I want you to give me Gabriel."

"Well, you see . . . an expert accountant is just a copy boy with numbers."

"I'll pay for his education, and then I'll give him a good salary."

"But he'll just be a bookkeeper. We wanted Gabriel to go to college. . . ."

"He can go and become a doctor of accounting."

"We don't know of any doctors of accounting. . . ."

Gabriel's destiny was resolved in a rather offhand way the day that the whole family got together: parents, grandparents, aunts, uncles, nieces, and nephews. The family stopped talking as they watched the boy doing acrobatics with some pickup sticks that came as a sales gimmick in the bottom of the crate that brought the adding machine.

In the spaces between the geranium pots, the boy had built a network of suspension bridges that were supported by some intricate calculations of balance, on top of which rose a structure that the adults qualified as a masterwork of engineering, when it was nothing more than the easiness of a steady hand, because there was no reason for the hand to be otherwise. Suddenly, without any discussion among the adults, who had gotten accustomed to celebrating to help lighten the weight of the stagnant hours, they all agreed: the boy wouldn't be a lawyer or an expert accountant; he would be an engineer. It was impossible not to see that he had an obvious vocation for it. After all, engineers also worked with numbers, and it was a profession that was starting to have some success in the sleeping city, which was beginning to stretch away from the mountains, carefully balancing itself along the edges of the canyons. The city kept getting bigger, and there were times when deaths kept even with births. The mothers invented many tricks to fool Death, leaving strangled puppies in roadside ditches dressed in their children's clothing so that Death would take them, believing they were human beings.

That day in the old house, the adults sealed the pact with a glass of wine that Aunt Clarita kept under lock and key for great occasions.

"Mama Chana, serve everyone a glass of wine!"

"But today isn't Easter, or anything like it."

"That's none of your business!"

"Fine, fine. . . ."

They made a toast and emptied their glasses while Aunt Catalina barely dampened her emaciated lips with the evil liquor that had the power to drag people from their homes and lead them down twisted pathways.

"To your health!"

"To Gabriel's health!"

"To Aunt Catalina's health!"

The adults made this pact while the boy entertained himself by picking his nose, unaware of the future his elders were planning for him.

The next day Aunt Catalina had a large amount of money deposited in the bank, destined to pay for the studies of the boy who had become her favorite nephew. Gabriel would go to Paris as soon as he was old enough, when the separation from his family wouldn't make the boy feel like a branch being lopped off a tree.

Bruna sat on the fountain, complaining:

"A boy can go to Paris or to the ends of the earth. He doesn't have a virginity to protect; he was born with the privilege of being a man. Meanwhile, she can't walk alone from the high school to her house, which is only a few blocks away. She was born with the stigma of being a woman, so she's condemned to the ghetto. Everyone who passes by is a threat to her virginity, even the birds that sit on the power lines, the trees with their long arms, the mountains when they play hide-and-seek and play tricks with the light, the rainbow and all the people and things that. . . ." (The adults lowered their voices to keep talking about all the things that the children shouldn't know about.)

The years went by, and Gabriel, who up until then had been a good student and had shown a certain affinity for numbers, went to the largest city in the world with his aunt's blessing, his father's advice, Bruna's envy, and a small bag full of gold coins. No sooner had he arrived, stammering and imitating the new language, than his eyes popped out of his head and were soon blinded by the light of all the new things. One by one the blindfolds fell off his eyes, his limbs shook off the apathy of *soroche,* and a distant taste of adventure made his mouth water. The same thing happened to him that had happened to his great-aunt Camelia the Tearful. And under these circumstances he became a tango singer overnight and ended his career as a student by marrying a Polish ballerina he met in a café in the Latin Quarter.

He was a caged lion who had broken through the bars and leapt into the jungle to shake his mane and test out his claws. He was champagne popping out of a bottle. He was the butterfly escaping the nets, breaking out of jail with the strength of its wings.

When the news reached the city, Aunt Catalina nearly died of shame and sorrow. With her hands trembling, she let out a cry to the heavens. Bruna's parents put the blame on the aunt; they cried a bit and realized that they had to pay her back to silence her complaints, which were splitting the rocks of the fountain. Aunt Catalina took the money and used it to pay for 315 Masses begging heaven for the salvation of the wayward lamb. All the brotherhoods and sisterhoods in the city chanted prayers of supplication. But in spite of all this, the boy didn't want to return to the fold: he kept on thinking that his ballerina's legs and the music that came from her body when she danced were the most beautiful things in the world.

Dear son:

We beg you with tears in our eyes not to fill us with dishonor and shame, and to leave ballerinas alone and come right home. . . .

Dear parents:

I regret to inform you that I'm not coming back, I'm going on tour with my wife. . . .

Dear nephew:

God knows how much you have made me suffer with your waywardness and your sins. I've said a novena to Saint Rita so that . . .

Dear aunt:

Do not suffer so. If you met my wife, you'd be amazed.

Dear brother:

Send me a photo of your wife right away, I'm dying to know
what she's like. There's nothing around here but a weeping and
wailing and gnashing of teeth. . . .

When the letter came addressed to Bruna, everyone held their
breath when they saw a beautiful young woman dressed in the
skimpiest clothing smiling at them from so far away and inviting
them to dance with her to an unknown and tempting rhythm. Aunt
Catalina climbed up on the pedestal of good reputation in order to
reach down and grab the photo with the force of a hurricane and tear
it into a thousand pieces that she threw down the well so that nobody would yield to the temptation of gluing them back together.

"Indecency! Obscenity! Contempt for heaven and this house's
good reputation!"

The Devil, in the bottom of the well, took it upon himself to put
the photo back together by moving his one eye around in a semi-
circle, and when the job was done and the pieces reattached to each
other, he was greatly surprised to see that this was a photo not of a
half-naked ballerina but of an old boot.

"Damn it! All that work for nothing!"

In Aunt Catalina's mind, deep within her cerebral membranes, in
the place where she formed opinions, she reached the verdict that
none of the members of the Catovil family had gone as far as her
nephew had. The supposed relations between her brother, Francisco,
and Mama Chana were a bunch of nonsense compared with this
scandal. Salomón Villa-Cató's 245 children were nothing compared
with what Gabriel had done. Not even Camelia the Tearful's defiant
acts: smoking with her long mother-of-pearl cigarette holder and filling the house's salon and drawing rooms with smoke and gallant
admirers. . . . Those things from the past were dead and buried, but
the news of Gabriel's marriage shook the foundations of the house,
and the fish in the fountain tried to cover its eyes with its fins: it was
such a toadying hypocrite.

They went through a period in which human values were shoved upside down and inside out into the trunks, where the people put what they couldn't bring themselves to throw out in the street. Everything was all mixed up in the trunks up in the attic. Even the homeowners couldn't find what they were looking for up there. Everything was covered with so much dust that you couldn't tell rheumatism from faith, cockroach feet from conventionalisms, beliefs from old shoes, love from yellowing old papers, and pain from rusty iron bars. The poor people were so blinded by their mania of keeping everything in big trunks that when they were looking for a moral obligation, they would find a useless knife handle instead.

"A ballerina is the most corrupt kind of woman there is. One can't even imagine a decent woman showing her legs."

In their daily lives it was possible to overlook lapses in honor and loyalty. Lying, stealing, slandering, were mistakes that were easy for any human to make, because there were moments when the hands or the tongue went their own way and nobody was responsible for what they did. . . . Over these mistakes one could spread a veil of pious understanding. But the mistakes that went against what they called shame, those that came even remotely near the carnal sins, those that damaged the family name, disturbed the great name, were unpardonable.

The fact that the ballerina had entered the family's clan was without precedent. The family put up an unbreachable wall of silence and tried to make the years go by more quickly, changing the topic whenever Gabriel's name came up.

"The shame, my God, the shame of it, a Catovil married to a ballerina!"

"Don't talk about Gabriel! Epiphany, the cat, is going to have kittens!"

Bruna had a fit when she saw Aunt Catalina tear up the photo and throw it into the well. She cried tears of sadness and rage. She felt as if she had found a friend who must be about the same age.

By the yellow moonlight, she saw in the mirror that her body was like the ballerina's and that, if she wanted to, she could grab hold of a ray of sunlight and twist it into a belt around her waist. But in the city she was condemned to wearing cheap clothes with long sleeves and collars that imprisoned her throat like a clamp and stockings held up by garters high up her leg that left a red mark that disgraced the flesh. She had to cover herself up as if her body were full of sores, or as if an evil being had tattooed obscene designs on her body, out of which flowed a fluid that drove one to sin.

"Life is too short to put up with so much crap."

So it read in tiny little letters at the entrance to the house, on one of the columns around the courtyard, and halfway up the stairs. It was a good thing that the aunts couldn't imagine that their nieces and nephews had dared to write on the walls, and that Mama Chana was nearsighted.

25

The young ballerina also had her story: her parents died during the war, and she was taken in by neighbors who put her into a convent as a novice. One day she heard Gypsy music at the foot of the convent's outer walls. She climbed up the wall to see what was happening and saw the Gypsies dancing. In that moment she guessed that the world was wide open, and without thinking twice, she yanked off the habit she was wearing, jumped over the wall, and joined the Gypsies to go dancing around the world with them—until the day she bumped into Gabriel and saw deep in his eyes a solitude so intense that she froze. Joining their destinies, they broke a pitcher and mixed a few drops of their blood, which they drew with the edge of a Gillette blade.

"No pain, or sickness, or war will ever separate us, until death. . . ."

This marriage astounded and alarmed the family who lived in the old house and the relatives who lived next door. Bruna wasn't a little girl anymore, ever since she had felt she wasn't alone in the world, and little by little she began to translate her ideas into words that drove her family up the wall; she gradually began to make plans for her life, knowing that in other places the possibility existed that her thoughts could become a reality without causing a scandal.

"If I knew that they wouldn't give me a beating, I'd go around the orchard naked."

"My God! Are you out of your mind?"

"I'm fed up with praying all the time!"

"Bruna, you're going to get yourself condemned!"

"To which hell?"

The clothes that she covered herself with filled her with shame. She wasn't in favor of nudism, but she thought that humanity still had a long way to go toward freeing itself from prejudices and the weight of conventionalisms that defiled human dignity and made people loathe the beauty of an adolescent body like the ballerina's, without their knowing why. There would be less distrust—she thought—if the sexual parts were regarded no differently from one's face or fingers. People should aspire to reach the point where a man could look at a naked woman without his mouth dropping open or his thoughts making his eyes turn what was really a table into a bed. . . . And a woman, coming across a man in the same condition, wouldn't run away or feel the least bit uncomfortable.

"Aren't you cold, señor?"

"No, señorita, I'm used to it."

The height of civilization would be reached when all people would be able to live their own lives the way they wanted to. And everyone would accept one another's tastes with a tolerance leaning more toward love than indifference, looking for the implications rather than the causes of the errors and weaknesses of others. They would never reach this point in the sleeping city, but it was still worth living, if only to try. Even Aunt Catalina herself would have been a different woman if they hadn't put the idea into her head that she should hate her miserable flesh so much.

A few years later the odd couple formed by Bruna's brother and the ballerina appeared in the sleeping city. He missed his house and family, who had placed so much hope in him, and she was curious to see the birthplace of the man who made her so happy.

They appeared unexpectedly one afternoon like a spring rain, and before they greeted their flabbergasted relatives, who grabbed the railing of the second-floor balcony to keep themselves from fainting with dismay, they asked for a hammer and chisel and started to demolish the hateful fish that was the symbol of the house;

164

when they had reduced it to a pile of rubble at the base of the fountain, they replaced it with the "pisstatue" that they had taken turns carrying from Brussels. When they finished installing it, and the statue of the little prince did what it was supposed to do on top of the fountain, the family remained flabbergasted and wanted the couple never to come back. Only Bruna celebrated the arrival of her brother and the "pisstatue."

Aunt Catalina had died shortly before. The fish no longer had a reason to be there. And since they were Gypsies without a home of their own, they at least wanted the house of their memories to have a quiet patio and the beautiful fountain to have a nicer spout.

The next day the couple grabbed their bags, which were very light now, and left the city, holding hands. Bruna gathered all the courage she could muster and went after them. The "pisstatue" stayed in the house, trying to work the miracle of bringing it back to life, but it was hopeless: the house had been abandoned to the domain of imps and ghosts. Only Aunt Clarita was left, calling out every five minutes to the nieces and nephews in the house next door to come over and spend some time with her. Like the grass growing between the stones in the patio, she survived only by great effort. The young people, including her numerous nieces and nephews, emigrated from the city toward life. They left trying to escape from the *soroche* that followed closely upon their heels.

26

Aunt Catalina didn't bathe very often because it made her so anxious. She never took off all her clothes. She was born wearing a white woolen smock that she made herself inside her mother's belly when her mother involuntarily swallowed some dust balls left behind by the carpet that covered the city for years. She kept the smock in the back of her closet, moistening it from time to time with rainwater and stretching it so that she could eventually use it as a shroud. She swore that she had never been naked in her life, and afraid that her guardian angel might happen to see her naked, she took the precaution of getting into the bathtub with her clothes on.

"No matter how much of an angel he is, one cannot permit oneself certain liberties in his saintly presence. . . ."

"But, Catalina, how can you think such unclean thoughts!"

"One thing I am *not* is shameless!"

She washed her private parts with an old sheepskin glove that was stiff from use. She detested touching her own skin. The dried-up glove was like a claw, streaking her whole body with red and purple lines, like a plow dragging across her skin, making furrows that she filled with the stale smell of dead flowers from the household soap.

With genuine mastery she took off her wet clothes at the same time that she put on dry ones, taking care not to expose the smallest part of her straggly and emaciated body. She left the bathroom, soaking wet and shivering, and sat in a shaft of sunlight, but the shaft of light bent away as it came in contact with her body. The wet clothing made her suffer the ill effects of abdominal rheumatism, but she held up bravely, as this was the price of not smelling like a goat. She left the bath with the sadness of a shy person who had fallen into the middle of a puddle.

"So much work, my God, just to die someday!"

Mama Chana dried her feet and cut her nails. She filed her calluses with a chunk of pumice and powdered them with rice starch. Without her feet she couldn't take her long daily walks. Annoyed by the children, who had been attracted by the curiosity of seeing their aunt's feet, she ordered the servant to put on her black stockings and high-heeled boots:

"Quick, quick, the *guambras* have picked up the scent like buzzards after dead meat!"

"Run, run, you can still see a piece of her heel!"

The kids had made a hole in the bathroom door to watch their aunt's maneuverings. Led by Bruna, they lined up and took turns spying on her, even though they already knew that they would never actually manage to see anything.

"She's taking off her girdle!"

"Now she's putting on her underwear!"

"Now she's resting!"

"My turn!"

It was ridiculous of her to shut the door and latch it: she could have bathed in the fountain of the central park, at the foot of the bishop's monument and in plain sight of everybody, and nobody would have figured out that she was bathing herself; they would have taken her for someone who hadn't looked where she was going, and after commenting about it to each other, they would have helped her out along with her stiff glove and her rosy-smelling soap.

"That poor old woman fell into the fountain. . . ."

Aunt Catalina kept getting thinner and thinner. She dried up even while she was alive, divesting herself of the hated flesh that was the cruel jaileress of her free-floating soul. She wore a hair shirt. The wounds left by hair shirt allowed the bad moods and tempers to escape that her mistreated liver could not process. The hair shirt was a wide strip of coarse cloth that she made herself to fit her own broomstick-thin measurements. She pierced it with a dozen hobnails with sharpened points. She put this girdle around her waist and wore it across her back with the help of some thick laces. Everyone knew when she was wearing the hair shirt because she was even more bitter than usual and went around on tiptoe with her lips clamped tightly together, as if she were walking on hot coals. Aunt Clarita's cats sensed it, their whiskers quivering, and were determined to stay far away from her boots. When she took off the hair shirt, she marched around as firmly as a general.

The air grew rancid with the smell of blood. When she took off the hair shirt and put it on the balcony railing to dry, a cloud of flies buzzed around it.

"Here come the flies! She's taken off the hair shirt!"

"Let's go see it!"

Their aunt angrily shooed the flies away without understanding that they didn't realize what the object that they were hovering over was. She sprinkled it with camphorated alcohol. The flies and nephews withdrew a few feet, then came back. When she got tired of chasing away the flies, she figured that the hair shirt's blood and pain had dried, and she folded it up, kissing it as if it were a religious relic, and kept it in the back of her closet, next to the wool smock in which she had come into the world and in which she hoped to leave it. The hair shirt stayed there until next time.

The family doctor, who played a very important role for the people in the house, had given himself the thankless task of taking care of the aunt's skinny, unknown, and almost transparent body. Seeing that she was slipping from his hands, and that his science failed when confronted with this bony skeleton, he resorted in desperation to asking a confessor for help. The two experts in body and soul, respectively, agreed that the aunt had to change her diet.

"She's killing herself! She's got anemia, arthritis, and cerebral arteriosclerosis."

"I am also worried; she has a scrupulous conscience and a foolish trust in God."

The doctor kept prescribing things every time he visited, out of some kind of professional sense of honor, instead of sending her on a trip, because he always kept a copy of the Hippocratic oath in front of him, in a gilded frame. And the other one was a little frightened to see that the things his penitent sinner had apparently done to her body had gone too far. . . .

Aunt Catalina ate sheep meat only once a month, on the first Saturday, had a small soft-boiled egg during the festivities for her favorite saints, and some cocoa on Easter and Christmas. The confessor chosen by the doctor, who was also the doctor's patient, told her to eat meat every day and drink cocoa every evening, which was the long-established custom of the people who lived in the sleeping city.

"You have to do it. You're not fulfilling the Sixth Commandment."

"The Sixth? What are you saying? Only the Fifth!"

"Fifth or Sixth, what difference does it make!"

So she started to make strange salads that were intended to counteract the lustful effects of the charcoal-broiled meat and the cocoa. Aunt Catalina said that flesh attracted flesh, and she didn't want to put hers in a sinful situation. Aunt Catalina's salads were made from rose petals that Mama Chana bought from the church vestries. The roses were then carried to the house in wicker baskets and into the kitchen. The roses weren't washed, so that they wouldn't lose the blessings that had fallen on them. They took off the petals with extreme care, plucking them like chickens. With a napkin they wiped off things that looked as though they might be bugs, spread them out on a serving dish, and flavored them with olive oil, salt, lime juice from the orchard, and, finally, a Lord's Prayer.

When he heard about all these goings-on the family doctor couldn't take it anymore and sent his patient on a long trip, closing the doors of his consultation room to her forever and handing her some highly inflated bills as compensation for all his unrequited efforts.

"And if you see that insufferably pious old woman around here again, tell her I'm not here, that I've died and gone to hell . . . !"

In spite of her family's and the doctor's predictions, the diet that the aunt had imposed upon herself wasn't all bad. Except for the abdominal cramps, from which she would never stop suffering, because she never stopped visiting dark, damp, and cold places, she had a strange energy and a surprising vitality for her age.

27

One day, the secretary whose every breath and footstep Aunt Catalina kept such a close watch on got tired of his job and of the emotional looks that Bruna lavished on him every afternoon in the form of a smile, which seemed like a strangely complicit act, and of other special niceties that drove him to the brink of feverish outbursts, and then nothing—in spite of that kiss in the orchard—and made an official announcement to the aunt that purgatory (with the exception of few unforeseeable cases) was completely and totally empty, and that in order to write up the total number of souls redeemed by her prayers, exclamations, and sacrifices, he would need a more advanced model of adding machine that hadn't been invented yet, since the machine he was using registered only five-figure numbers, which made his job very difficult and therefore unpleasant. In reality, the poor young man was deathly tired of his boss and of all the Catovils. The aunt paid him the agreed-upon salary and said goodbye to him with a mixture of pain and relief.

"So, you're leaving us. . . ."

"Yes, señora."

"Señorita!"

"Yes, Señorita Catalina."

"Well then, may your guardian angel go with you always."

"I'm twenty years old, and I don't need a guardian angel, señora!"

"Señorita! Señorita! Show some respect!"

Faced with the dilemma of doing battle alone with the adding machine and the numbers, she understood that her end was near. She had done so much in this world that there was nothing left for her to do, except for one thing that she had always wanted: to visit Rome and the Holy Land (the part about Rome was inherited from her great-uncle Alvarito). She also had her doubts about the figures that the secretary had presented to her, and she lay awake thinking: There may still be some souls left in purgatory. . . . I may have gotten out only twenty or thirty thousand. . . . Maybe purgatory is just as full as ever. . . .

So, because of these doubts, she decided to make the trip. She had lived for nearly eighty years of deprivation and punishment when she started to make the preparations that were the prelude to her definitive trip to eternity. She would go to the holy places, visit the pope, and when she returned she would sit in the rocking chair on the patio, in front of the fountain, until death took her immaculate soul from the impure shell of her body.

"But Aunt Catalina, that's so far away. . . ."

"It doesn't matter, I must go like the Crusaders did!"

"But they were men, and they could ride horses. . . ."

"Even so, I will go alone! First by train and then by ship and with the help of God and all of his holy saints, I will get to where I must get to."

"Aunt, at your age . . ."

"The flesh is weak, but the spirit is strong!"

And so it was done. She spared no expense and packed her bags. She didn't allow anyone to go with her, claiming that she needed to be alone to collect herself. She made out her will, which was the custom of the people in the city when they were going to leave it, and she said good-bye to her astonished friends and family, who accompanied her to the train station, waving handkerchiefs that fanned their whispered words and one or two tears reserved for just such occasions.

"You should have seen the crazy old woman!"

"It runs in the family, it's in the blood."

"They might carpet the whole city again!"

"Don't say it so loud!"

The train that would take her to the other side of the mountains and then to the sea came forth triumphantly. She was carrying a big suitcase with all the clothes that she would need, her finest dress and shawl, and a small suitcase with her hair shirt and the final reports of indulgences earned and the grand total of souls she had gotten out of purgatory. During the trip, the motion of the train made the numbers change places. The words and prayers got so shaken up that they broke apart, and by the end of the trip the letters and numbers were so mixed up that they practically formed a new language. . . .

It was the first time that Aunt Catalina had made a long trip and left the mysterious heart of the city. Her sister, Clara, the only one who was crying inconsolably, calmed down a little seeing her military bearing and the composure with which she sat in the compartment she had reserved. The train gave one last whistle blast that pierced the clouds, echoed back and forth, and scattered along the flanks of the mountains. Then it left, limping along the railway line, carrying the aunt who did not stop waving her linen handkerchief; and when she disappeared around the first curve, the sun deflated, the imps high up on the rooftops took off their hats, and the people who had accompanied her with their heads fixed in the direction of the train, watching the column of smoke rising from the locomotive, returned their heads to their normal positions and spat out the lump that had gotten stuck in their throats.

"She's gone!"

"Oof, what a relief!"

"When will the poor thing reach the Holy Land?"

"What 'poor thing'? She wants to do this!"

"Let's go, Clarita, let's go. There's nothing to do here on the platform. . . ."

Aunt Catalina was euphoric, looking out the train window and seeing how the houses, trees, hills, and animals were running alongside her to the Holy Land and how the *chuga-chuga* of the train sounded exactly like the *ora-pro-no-bis* of her invocations.

She got through the first three-quarters of the train trip without any major mishaps, sleeping, praying, feeling a slight twinge of abdominal rheumatism every time a cloud of dust filtered through the poorly closed windows. After three days of going up and down mountains in the train, the aunt lost her patience.

"It's all for God! But how much longer? . . ."

Upon reaching the crucial point of the trip, which the passengers had thought about and feared in advance, the train panted and puffed, swallowing wood and spitting out fire. The passengers trembled. . . . The train had reached the limits of the strength of iron, crankshafts, and boilers. Nerves, backsides, and abdomens had reached the boiling point. They were coming to the place where the Devil lay waiting for the train to tickle his nose and make him blow a sneeze into the air.

"Passengers, get out! We've reached the Devil's Nose!"

"Holy Mother of All Suffering, this is where the trains derail!"

"María, hold on to the children. We're at the Devil's Nose."

"Jesus, how horrible!"

Aunt Catalina, seeing the precipices, the canyons accessible only to goats and not to humans, the loading and unloading of passengers so that the train, with its load lightened, could make it up the towering peak, the painful sound of overworked engines grinding away to haul the train by the nose and push it by the tail, the weary pilgrimage of the people behind the train, from where you could see it dangling over the edge of nothingness, managed to jump back toward the rocks, where she insisted that all the travelers kneel down and say, in unison, the prayer of the Just Judge.

"Pray, you heretics!"

The spirit of Girolamo Savonarola, the fiery Dominican monk, left his tomb and slipped into the aunt's sweaty clothes, becoming enclosed in her skirt, her flat chest, and her nose. The poor people had prayed a great deal, and all they wanted to do was get through the accursed pass and reach their destination alive. They were unwilling, and Aunt Catalina, seeing that the procession wasn't following her, that her fellow travelers weren't even paying attention to her, planted herself in the middle of the tracks, on her knees with her arms held out in a cross, ready to have the train ride over her bones.

"I'm not moving from this spot! Bad, ungrateful Christians! To go through what we just went through and not want to give thanks to heaven!"

"But, señora, the train whistle is blowing!"

"Señorita! Now pray, you heretic!"

The tired passengers looked at her with surprise. Night was coming fast, and with it a million lidless eyes started to fly around and get caught in the women's clothing and in their hair. The rocks opened up with an "open sesame" spoken by the shadows, and strange thoughts came to rest on their backbones, making them shiver with fright. Kneeling to pray wasn't enough, it was necessary to dig one's nails into God's heels, and the poor people of the train, pushed along by terror, may have done it already. So when they saw the aunt's pose, they looked at one another and all decided that she was a crazy old woman, and without further commentary they lifted her into the air and put her in a third-class carriage. The final all-aboard whistle blows made them rush, so they didn't realize that Aunt Catalina had fainted.

"The train's going! Hurry!"

"Lift up the crazy old woman!"

"So help us!"

"But she doesn't weigh anything!"

They finally reached the ocean. It was very hot, and the people gradually got used to the climate. Aunt Catalina, having recovered from the outrage recently committed against her, about which she guessed more than she knew, returned to her compartment at the next station stop and saw to her great irritation that her traveling companions were gradually stripping off their clothes.

"*Ave María Purísima!* Such disorder, and you're practically naked!"

"Aren't you hot, señora?"

"Se-ño-ri-ta!"

The air was humid and stifling. Through the windows of the train you could see people dressed in brightly colored clothing made with very little fabric. The aunt longed for the streets of the distant city, with its people dressed eternally in black. These people seemed to be from another planet: their skin was different, their eyes were different, their voices were different, their hips were different. The women didn't wear stockings, and their blouses opened to where one couldn't look without blushing. In sum, the men and women of this place must all be relatives of Satan.

"What am I supposed to do, surrounded by all this madness?"

"This way, señora, this way. That's your ship."

"Se-ño-ri-ta!"

"I'll carry your bags for you!"

"Don't you dare touch my bags!"

"But, señora, that's your ship."

"Se-ño-ri-ta!"

A big ship was waiting for her. It didn't sink into the sea because it was held up by sharks' fins. She boarded it on a gangplank that was swaying over the black water.

"This way, señora."

"Señorita! And don't touch me!"

When she got on deck with her suitcases, her umbrella, and her astonishment, she wanted to abandon the pilgrimage and go back to the sleeping city. She needed the peacefulness of her city and her house. Her fellow travelers were horrible people, the men didn't bow when she passed by, and the women were half naked. . . .

"What on earth is this! By Saint Stanislas of Kostka! Where am I?"

The heat gradually increased, and she was dressed all in black, absorbing the full intensity of the sun's rays and sticking out like a black peppercorn that had fallen into a fruit salad. A sticky sweat covered her whole body. She kept hearing her nieces and nephews yelling and the cats meowing. Completely dazed by the loud conversations, the ship's horn, and all the good-byes and adioses from people who were going on a one-way trip, never to return, she stood there, unable to do anything. . . .

Someone took hold of her and brought her to a tiny stateroom that, in addition, she had to share with the strangest being of all the ones she had seen up until then. The moment she saw her she resolved never to direct a single word toward her, not even in the event of a shipwreck. She was a large woman wearing a short dress that barely covered her and even showed the lines of her underpants. She was shameless, and she smoked like a man. Aunt Catalina remembered the mother-of-pearl cigarette holder that was in one of the cupboards in her house and started saying the prayer for a "good death":

"When my eyes are glazed and wild with the fear of death . . . When my pale and blackening face causes pity and terror . . . When my limbs are stiff and cold . . . Merciful Jesus, have compassion for me!"

The helpful, smiling stewards settled her into her stateroom, laid her bags on the bunk bed, and held out their hands, expecting a tip; in her confusion, she shook their hands weakly, then plunged herself into a sea of conjectures that was darker than the one beneath the boat. She was filled with discouragement. The sultry afternoon heat galloped heavily across her skin, but she remained faithful to her customs and refused to take off any of her clothes. She would never betray her principles. Besides, it was too late to turn back; she had to withstand whatever came her way, she had to be brave like the Crusaders of old. So she dedicated herself to hanging images of saints all over the stateroom; they would be her true and only traveling companions, since she had yet to see anyone who looked as though they had the required aptitude for a trip to the Holy Land. It was going to be a long trip, and she would have to make it alone.

She remembered her friends in the distant city and fanned herself with her thoughts. She started to pray mechanically:

"To make myself agreeable in thy sight, sprinkle me with holy water and I shall be purified. Thou shalt wash me and make me whiter than the mountain snow. . . ."

The ship set sail. The sea breeze calmed everyone's spirits, and it began to get cooler. Aunt Catalina went up on deck, holding on to the walls to keep herself from falling over from the ship's rolling. The spectacle up there was beautiful and imposing: the sea was calm, and the sky was filled with stars. She said her prayers, holding tight to the ship's railing while the wind undid her three-piece hair clasp. A bell rang. It was suppertime: she had to go down to the dining room, even though she didn't feel like eating.

When she got to the dining room she was seized by new afflictions: the place was a den of truly cardinal sins, for here in the flesh was the world with all its obscenities; lust and lechery were holding hands, gluttony and lewdness reigned supreme. She couldn't tolerate the spectacle that assailed her eyes. She had been tricked. This ship wasn't taking anyone to the Holy Land, it was going to hell, and there she was, all alone with her valise full of numbers and account statements, which was her passport to heaven. She couldn't bear to look any longer; as a form of silent protest, and so as not to be contaminated by the environment, she had two spoonfuls of soup, a scrap of bread, and one swallow of metallic-tasting water to keep down the protests and comments that were already halfway past her larynx. She got up and went to her stateroom with her umbrella and her desolation.

It was still very hot there. In spite of that, she lay down fully clothed, afraid that her traveling companion might come in at any moment and catch her in her underwear. She tried to sleep, tired and alienated by the sudden change in her life, the noise of the machines in her head (the hammer bone in her ear had gone crazy, banging away incessantly at the anvil), the noise of the waves breaking on the ship's keel, the nonstop rolling that made the saints' images tilt back and forth on the walls, and the feeling that a shipwreck was imminent.

At midnight her roommate came in, bringing the scent of alcohol with her. She said good night in some halting language, and the aunt, not wanting to break the wall of silence by answering, pretended to be asleep; the woman took advantage of this and took off what little clothing she was wearing, leaving herself completely naked. Then she began a strange ritual—a complicated late-night toilette that started with removing her hair, revealing a completely bare head with gray spots like a pigeon's egg. Then she took out her teeth and put them in a glass of water, precisely the glass that the aunt was supposed to use. She put her hand under her right eye, and with a sudden movement of her eyelid a glass eye appeared in her palm, a clear blue crystal ball through which she looked at the things in the world as if they were weightless, not even bound by the laws of gravity. She hummed while she did this, so as not to wake her sleeping roommate.

"Tralali-lali-laraa. . . ."

Aunt Catalina began her calculations, and when she figured that the woman was in her nightgown, she opened her eyes and discovered the imponderable nakedness of her being hairless, eyeless, toothless, topless, and shameless. She was petrified with terror and grew pale, feeling the true cold of death climbing up on her and squatting over her heart. It took a long time for her to recover; she drew strength from places that didn't have any and tried to conquer her astonishment and repugnance: the marrow in her bones had turned to water, her vocal cords were all tangled up. Her dignity abused and offended, she pulled the sheet over her head and shouted thunderously:

"Impure, impure liar! Spawn of Satan and of hell!"

And she collapsed into a stupor.

The woman couldn't understand a word, and thinking that she had asked her to turn out the light, she complied by getting quickly into the opposite bunk, displaying to the dismayed aunt a flabby and disgraceful butt that belonged to a bit of postwar scrap matériel, since she was a lieutenant on vacation who, in her distant youth, had suffered the consequences of the First World War. Before falling asleep Aunt Catalina heard, over and over:

"Tralali-lali-laraa . . ."

This macabre scene, so real and so promiscuous, made Aunt Catalina lose her head completely and made the roommate ask for a cabin change the next day.

The aunt was seasick for most of the voyage, doing backflips on the swordfish, blasting out of her room when the ship's horn blew as they passed very near the place where the pieces of María Illacatu's soul had been when her children took off their shirts on the high seas. Then she crawled into her shell to become a pearl, which was a relief for the rest of the passengers, who were sick of her meddlesome ranting and raving.

"The old woman with the umbrella hasn't shown up this morning."

"I hope she never does!"

One fine day she felt better, recovered her shaky senses, and left the bottom of the ocean, which for her was located under the fountain in the patio of her house, and tried to start up a conversation with a lady who had smiled at her as she passed by:

"It's a fine day, isn't it?"

"*Ich nicht verstehe.*"

"Excuse me?"

"*I don't understand.*"

"What did you say?"

"*Io non capito.*"

"Whaaaat?"

She averted her eyes and realized to her horror that nobody spoke her language. Panic filled her, and she believed that God was punishing all the shamelessness, insanity, and nudism by confounding their languages: the punishment of the Tower of Babel was about to repeat itself, any minute the sailors wouldn't be able to understand the captain's orders, and there would be chaos on the high seas, among the sharks' pointy teeth and the sperm whales' humps. . . .

Full of holy wrath, she stood in the middle of the deck and started to preach and to call the voyagers to repentance. For the second time, the spirit of Brother Savonarola crawled under her skin and came out through her eyes and her mouth.

"Sinful men and women! Repent your sins immediately! God has confounded our languages! Repent! We're going to sink!"

People looked at her, bothered and confused. This strange creature dressed all in black, wielding her umbrella like a weapon, was making the crossing disagreeable. The aunt kept on preaching and shouting until she was hoarse. The tourists rushed to take pictures of this. The children started to circle around them, clapping their hands, thinking there was a circus on board. The seagulls froze in midflight, landing on the mainmast. Two or three people who spoke her language understood the word "shipwreck," and believing that she was a religiously enlightened being, they fainted. Terror spread throughout the ship, which turned sharply, because the engineer understood that someone had fallen into the sea. The ship's horn blew rapidly and crazily, and the passengers came up on deck with their eyes bugging out and life vests on their backs. The captain intervened, being the last one likely to lose his head, and figured out that the source of all the confusion was the old woman with the umbrella. So he ordered the ship's doctor to put her in a straitjacket, inject her with a powerful dose of narcotics, and take her to the infirmary. She spent the rest of the trip there.

"At last we'll have a peaceful trip!"

"The old woman with the umbrella is locked up."

"What a relief!"

And so the voyage went on for nearly a month. It was the longest and most senseless month of her life. She spent it putting on and taking off her hair shirt, saying very long prayers in which she confused the usual words with strange sounds, talking the whole time to keep herself company, cursing the wicked people in the world

181

who were crazy enough to believe that this absurd form of travel would get them to the Holy Land. The voyage that she had always dreamed of was something else completely; she believed that the pilgrims would travel seated on rows of benches as in a church, praying and singing pious psalms, while the sea breeze caressed their hair and the fish accompanying them on their crossing formed beautiful designs in the clear blue crystal.

When she returned from her trip she was stark raving mad and determined to die. Her friends, nieces and nephews, and the rest of her family who were anxiously awaiting her return didn't hear about any of this and remained ignorant of all these goings-on. She did bring back two suitcases full of rosaries and medallions that the travel agency gave her as they put her on the train that would take her back to the city. But her body never even reached the Holy Land or passed through Rome.

The captain, the sailors, and the other passengers on the ship couldn't stand her anymore, and they left her shut in a cheap hotel and picked her up on the way back, after giving her the proper dose of narcotics.

In response to the persistent questions from her closest friends and family who wanted to know what the places were like that she had gone to visit, poor Aunt Catalina could only manage to say, holding her head in her hands:

"Two hundred fourteen Avenue de la Rambla, third floor, right, Barcelona, Spain!"

"Yes, what happened there?"

"Nothing, nothing. Two hundred fourteen Avenue de la Rambla, right, third floor, Barcelona, Spain."

That was all she got out of her long-awaited trip. She had lost all her luggage, along with the only expensive dress she ever had in her life, which she had ordered made to fit her emaciated frame to wear during her interview with the pope; she had lost the largest and most beautiful shawl that she could find in the city, which she had bought for the same purpose, and also the umbrella that she was never without, and the suitcase with all the reports of her indulgences earned and the grand total of souls that she had managed to get out of purgatory.

"Aunt Catalina, where did you leave your luggage?"

"Two hundred fourteen Avenue de la Rambla, third floor, right."

"Catalina, try to remember."

"Avenue . . ."

The truth was that she never left Barcelona. She stayed there in a cheap hotel, taken care of, or rather badly taken care of, by some charitable souls, until the sailors came to get her for the return voyage, where they put her back in the ship's infirmary and then placed her in a sealed compartment on the train, until she arrived in the city on the correct date. The people who were waiting for her stood there with their mouths open when they saw her with her hair all disheveled, her eyes staring wildly, and without her umbrella. . . .

Once the rosaries and medallions had been distributed to the city folk who rushed over to pay her compliments and to pry, she lay down in her big bed and never got up again.

28

Aunt Catalina's bed was a masterpiece of art. It was a genuine wooden monument that rose and fell along with the tormented and twisted imagination of an artist named Juanico, who worked hard but suffered more pain when he listened to the sad Indian songs that they played at the door to his studio while he shaped and polished the wood.

The bed was made out of four life-size statues, carved out of cedar wood, representing the four evangelists, their heads supporting four large carved wooden beams that held up a hanging purple canopy.

This was Aunt Catalina's only luxury, although she thought of it as a necessity. It was the only bed of its kind in the city, possibly in the world. The four evangelists—Saints Matthew, Mark, Luke, and John—had come down from heaven itself to observe the aunt's troubled sleep. They were covered with sheets of gold foil that had been painted, since there was so much gold in the city that it could easily be used as a base to make the brushes glide better.

The four apostles were condemned to staying in the aunt's bedroom, not even going out for a bit of sun, until she died. It was a bed fit for a pope, proud, imposing, which any mortal person who was not the aunt would have felt guilty about lying down upon. But the mattress was miserable; it was made with stiff, cold straw from the high, windy plains, full of icy thorns that pierced the skin right through to the bones. It was an austere bed, hard and solemn, where the ghosts organized processions and the imps played hopscotch during the day; and when night fell and the aunt climbed between the sheets, they entertained themselves by tiptoeing over her body from head to toe. When the aunt rolled over, they lost their balance and fell with their legs in the air, which made them angry enough to give her a thrashing, but the aunt never noticed what the imps were doing: she had mastered her body like the fakirs of India.

It took Juanico many years to finish the bed. The music that played while he worked shaping the wood got inside him until he became sick with *soroche*. Then he spent whole days not doing anything, with his head in his hands, looking at the hemp sandals on his feet.

Aunt Catalina went to his studio and, jabbing him under the arms with the tip of her umbrella, forced him to his feet and urged him to finish the job.

"Juanico, you loafer! When are you finishing my bed? Laziness is the mother of all vices!"

"That's how it is. . . ."

"This is the end! I've been waiting for two years!"

"I'll be done soon. . . ."

"Juanico, I need my bed!"

"Soon, soon. . . ."

"If you don't deliver it by Corpus Christi, I won't pay you for it! Do you understand?"

"Okay. . . ."

"And I'll also have you put in jail for swindling."

"Okay. . . ."

The morning it was due, Juanico was found dead next to the bed.

"Catalina, Juanico is dead!"

"If he hasn't finished my bed, he must be in hell."

"Poor Juanico, who is no more!"

Saint Mark's right foot was still rough, as if he hadn't finished walking through his mother's womb the nine months that he was shut in, and the left one was still inside the unpolished wood. Saint

185

Luke's hair was ocher because the gold leaf hadn't been burnished enough by the angels' wings—because the angels got bored with the task and abandoned the artist, thinking that it was stupid for such a bed to go to an overpious old maid. There were other faults, as there were in many artistic works of the period, since they were started by fathers and finished by grandchildren; but amid the grandeur of the total work, they went unnoticed.

Aunt Catalina's bed was completed by one of Juanico's descendants. But this one wasn't as skilled as his predecessor, and above all, his soul wasn't twisted like Juanico's, so that the carving style of the headboard that he had to finish wasn't anything like the solemn style of the four evangelists, those four severe and majestic statues. The headboard was carved in a different style, depicting two little angels playing with a garland of flowers. The little angels' bodies were graceful and full of life, as if they had really been carved out of a celestial block of wood. But this delicious pair had a serious drawback according to the aunt's taste: you could see the little angels' *pipís,* and she would never tolerate "that" on her headboard.

"How dare you put nudity in my bed!"

"So what do you want me to put?"

"A saint or something, like in the agreement with your grandfather Juanico."

"That's why I put the angels."

"But you shouldn't have made them the way they came into the world!"

"And who says they've come into the world?"

"Lower your voice! Insolence! Blasphemy!"

The aunt had no choice but to accept the bed as it was, and once it was installed in her bedroom, she dedicated herself to making underwear for the little angels, which she attached to the wood with strips of paper and glue. But the nieces and nephews couldn't resist tearing off the strips of paper so that they could enjoy the spectacle of their aunt bursting out of there, her face red with shame and indignation, looking for another change of clothing every time one disappeared.

In spite of the 425,822 centuries of indulgences that she had accumulated, Aunt Catalina did not die peacefully. She suffered for weeks, and it would have gone on longer if Mama Chana, tired from so much fussing, hadn't given her the "tea of mercy" that she prepared in such cases.

"She's been in agony for days and days. . . ."

"She's turning the house upside down and driving the family crazy. . . ."

"I'm going to give her a little 'tea of mercy'!"

"Make it quickly! After all, you're doing her a favor. . . ."

The aunt wanted to confess every five minutes. The priests and the members of the sisterhoods that she belonged to moved into the old family house to live. The aunt didn't want to be left alone even for a moment because she was afraid that Death would lift her into the air like the people on the train, or like the sailors on the ship, and carry her off when she wasn't even dead yet. Her mind was in chaos; she was afraid of falling victim to the sharks who came in and out of the door to her room, who climbed up the pillars of the four apostles onto her bed, carrying the suitcase with the papers that documented all of her accumulated indulgences.

"All is well, my daughter, you may confess. . . ."

"I confess that I have seen a shark. . . ."

"That's not a sin, my daughter."

"I confess that I let the ship's captain put his hands on me. . . ."

"I already told you—"

"I confess that I lost my suitcase."

"That's not a sin, either."

"I confess that . . . Two hundred fourteen Avenue de la Rambla, third floor, right. . . ."

"Rest, my daughter, rest."

"No, don't go! Don't leave me alone!"

Aunt Clarita was worn out with fatigue and overwhelmed with pain. In spite of everything, she loved her sister and felt that she was losing a big part of her life. The dreams that would be shared no longer were crumbling, the joys and sorrows wouldn't be spread on the tablecloth during the long after-dinner chats they had with each other. She would sit alone in front of the fire that they would light during the endless afternoon rains. She stayed alone in the enormous house, where she wandered lost among the innumerable rooms, and where she became old, and where the ghosts lost all secrecy and modesty and did whatever they wanted to even in broad daylight: if they felt like having bread and jam, they ate some and left the blackberry-smeared knives and spoons lying all over the table. They sat in the rocking chairs in the courtyard and didn't even move over when someone sat on top of them. They crawled inside the cats' noses and came out disguised as ferocious howls. They drank all the water in the fountain and left it dry for days. They poked around the remains of the third floor, slid down the gutters, and swung from the spiderwebs. . . .

Mama Chana used Aunt Catalina's trip abroad as an excuse to come take possession of the house, and under the pretext of accompanying Aunt Clarita, she settled in, waiting for the two aunts to die so that she could die and leave the house to her children.

"Doña Catalina has finally died!"

"May she rest in peace!"

"Let's go grab something of hers to keep as a holy relic!"

"Let's do it quickly! The room is full of people."

As soon as the aunt was dead the bells began to toll, and everyone in the city formed a procession toward the Catovils' house. The aunt's room was left in shambles. Everyone took a souvenir of her sainthood with them: a flower vase where she had offered Castilian roses to Saint Benito; one of the slippers that she used for walking around on her knees; a feather from the pillow where she had lain, thinking her heavenly thoughts; a brick from the wall that had witnessed the daily mortifying of her own flesh; a piece of the bed-

spread, a bit of clothing, a few loose threads from one of the sheets.
. . . They took everything they could grab. They took down the purple canopy and divided it up. When the four evangelists were freed from the heavy beams they were carrying, they shook off the dust that had covered them, stretched, and walked out into the street arm in arm until they found some hidden corner of the sacristy of the principal church, where they remained for years until someone discovered them and put them in an altarpiece.

"I've seen that saint somewhere. . . ."

"Me too, but I don't remember where. . . ."

"I don't know who made it, or where it came from. . . ."

The rooms on the second floor were closed off, definitively and forever. Aunt Clarita was tired of going up and down the stairs. So she gave up the second floor to the ghosts on the condition that they leave her alone and not come down to the patio, where she was trying to spend her remaining years. But the ghosts proliferated, and after a few years she had to pay them rent just to have a couple of rooms to herself.

The garden was a mess, completely taken over by garbage and weeds. Nobody bothered to pick the lemons from the trees or to sit in the shadow of the old cherry tree and eat its fruits; the well with the eye of the Devil was in ruins, and nobody went near it anymore to see what was at the bottom.

When Aunt Clarita sat in the shadow of the "pisstatue" to get some sun and comb her hair, the little imps pulled her hairs out one by one, then put them back in, but as they touched them the hairs turned white, and many of them got lost while they were playing this game. . . .

29

Aunt Clarita had her feet on the ground, and she walked around softly on it, although she sometimes got lost in the labyrinth of her own house. She was the opposite of her sister; she had delicate bones, with skin that needed care and pampering; she was refreshed by red blood that flowed in and out of a tender heart; and she fought desperately against the *soroche* every morning just to be able to get out of bed with the first rays of sunlight.

She loved her nieces and nephews, her cats and her plants. She was extraordinarily beautiful, so much so that she examined every part of her body with a magnifying glass to see if her pores were clogged with dust and if her soft, tiny hairs were straight. She was still a little flirtatious, a habit left over from the days when she had a number of suitors whom Aunt Catalina took charge of sweeping away with the stiff broom of her scathing remarks. Catalina found a way to leave hydrangeas wherever Aunt Clarita might touch them and so remain single. Aunt Catalina loved her sister, in her own way. She wanted her to be by her side always, on earth and in heaven, and she wasn't about to let a little thing like marriage keep her out of the chorus of Eleven Thousand Virgins that she believed in so literally.

With decisive and irrefutable arguments, she objected to her forming a bond with one of the men prowling around the house. Sometimes she said that the suitor didn't have the Catovils' noble lineage, because she had seen with her own eyes that the lover's family tree had some prickly nettle growing around its base and that dogs came near it and lifted their legs. . . .

"Are you crazy? You're going to marry a *cholo?*"

"He's not a *cholo!*"

"Shut up, you don't know anything!"

Sometimes she scratched one of the men hanging around the house with her fingernail to get a small skin sample and found evidence of Indian blood, biologically incompatible with the blood of the Catovils. . . .

"He is not of your rank!"

"It doesn't matter! He wants to marry me."

"Don't be a fool! His grandmother was an Indian, I knew her, she used to wear a headdress."

"But—"

"Forget it! That one's not setting foot in this house again."

Sometimes she made it her task to lift up the lover's frock coat, using just her eyes, and discovered that under the frock coat, which had been cut to measure by the best tailor in the city, was a multi-colored poncho.

"Believe it or not, he's pure Indian. . . ."

Other times she was certain that the one who was seeking Aunt Clarita's hand didn't even have a grave to drop dead in. She said that his shoes didn't even match, that his shirt collar had a tear that had been sewn up, that he wore tin-plated buttons, one of which was missing from his vest, that his big toe was sticking out through a hole in his sock. . . .

"That one wants to marry you because he thinks you're rich."

"That's not true!"

"He just wants your money."

"But, since I don't have any . . ."

"He's a fortune hunter. If I see him around here, I'll drive him out with the broomstick!"

Other times she was sure that the suitor's pants didn't fit right, and she said that he was a piece of spun sugar who would crumble at the first bite. That he would be incapable of giving her any moral support, because when she wanted to lean on him they would both end up rolling on the ground, since the boyfriend's morality was as fragile as a paper bag.

"How can you marry that joker? Don't you see how ridiculous he is?"

"No, no, he isn't!"

"He couldn't even walk the dogs. . . ."

"But—"

"Why do you want to get married so badly? You should take cold baths instead."

"Catalina! Don't think such improper thoughts. . . ."

She also said that one suitor was ugly and that when the first child was born, poor Aunt Clarita would suffer such a shock from seeing her son's face that she would die after childbirth.

"With a man like that? Jesus, how scary!"

"Why?"

"Because he looks like the evil spawn of Satan!"

Lots of times she said that the suitor didn't go to Mass, that he belonged to the Liberal Party, that the Liberals had been sworn enemies of the family since the days of Bishop Catovil, and she accused the innocent girl in love of betraying the family.

"Clara, you might as well smack me in the face! That one is our worst enemy."

"That's not true!"

"If you marry him, you'll bring disgrace to this house."

"But, if he's so good—"

"How can he be good—an atheist who doesn't go to Mass!"

Aunt Catalina's arguments were the same ones that had been repeated in the city from time immemorial, and they kept repeating them in Bruna's day when they didn't approve of the children marrying someone of their own choosing but gratefully welcomed the husband and wife who had been selected in accordance with the social rank they had been stuck in arbitrarily.

192

Finally Aunt Clarita, tired of primping in front of the mirror, of sighing at the open windows, understood that it was her destiny to have a long, sad spinsterhood in which the cats would take the place of children and geranium leaves that of diapers lying out to dry in the flower pots in the courtyard. She understood that the road that led to kisses was forbidden to her forever. She resigned herself to the fate of her older sister's rule, but she remained unconvinced, and continued to dream, and to read ever-so-slightly-spicy little novels, and to engage in a few other childish coquetries that helped her kill the long, dead hours of her life and fill the holes in her loneliness. She lacked Camelia the Tearful's determination and the opportunity to feed on different air that didn't carry the burden of *soroche*.

Aunt Clarita was small. Her eyes were watery and bright like two puddles of rain. Blue veins crisscrossed her hands like streams on a map, marking the desolate landscape that one could walk through and go nowhere. She managed to sidestep a year or two of mourning in the long chain of deaths in the family by wearing brightly colored clothes that lit up the old house and marked off the alleged seasons of winter and summer. She allowed herself a few freedoms behind her sister's back, looking through fashion magazines and heaving sighs that steamed up the pages. She subscribed to *Au Bon Marché* from Paris, which arrived from time to time and gave her the chance to make furtive trips beyond the mountains.

She used large amounts of 4711 cologne. She wore silk stockings, and when she got ready to go out into the street to show off her unused charms, she spent far too much time on the meticulous, tedious process of getting all fixed up, which drove everyone else in the house crazy.

She made beauty masks to slow down the passing years and wipe the wrinkles from her face. She put egg white in a little corn flour and beat it vigorously, then put the mixture on her face, neck, and just below with a flat wooden blade. Unlike all other women, Aunt Clarita did all of her beauty mixtures and cleansings in full view of everyone and enjoyed it.

"Clara, show some modesty. It's a bad example for the children!"

"Why?"

"Because vanity is a very serious sin."

"Stop saying such silly stuff!"

"Remember that from dust you came and to dust you shall return."

When the paste on her skin dried it became as stiff as a plaster statue; she couldn't talk or make any movements at all. She spoke with her hands and eyes, and the nieces and nephews followed her everywhere, trying to make her laugh so that the mask would crack open.

"Aunt Clari-i-ita, give us a smi-i-ile, so the ma-a-ask will break."

Then she removed it very carefully, washing herself with rainwater in which she had boiled lettuce leaves that she picked from the garden herself.

"Aunt Clarita, let me touch your face!"

"Fine, but wash your hands first."

And one by one the children would touch her face with the tips of their fingers.

"Wow, it's so soft!"

"Like petting a cat!"

"Soft and fresh!"

She painted her lips a vivid red in the style of Betty Boop; she enlarged her eyes with a charcoal pencil and dyed her hair reddish blond—using peroxide—with tiny curls that snuggled up to her eyebrows and temples, making her look like a poodle.

None of this was looked upon with pleasure by her ferocious sister, who, after having plunged her into solitude, forever pursued her about the house with the same old serenade as always:

"Clara, Clara, you're going to get yourself condemned! Remember that from dust you came and to dust you shall return!"

And when she managed to leave the house through the false door, she kept hearing the same refrain. Her sister had figured out a way of hiding in her parasol, inside her purse, or her favorite place, in the curly spirals nearest to her ear.

Aunt Clarita had few friends because she painted her face, which had the wrong effect, and because of the number of suitors she had to turn away, who, feeling themselves slighted in any way, dedicated themselves to spreading rumors that the women took as given and practically affirmed that she had fallen, knowing all the time that Aunt Catalina's constant presence and spying had prevented so much as a kiss on the fingertips.

Aunt Clarita hated the hypocrisy of the customs that enveloped the sleeping city. She was the second edition of Camelia the Tearful, without having had her wonderful opportunities. She bore her loneliness with integrity and spiritual elegance, without complaining or posing as a victim, as if deep inside she felt that she was guilty of not sending her sister to the Devil while there was still time to do it. She had a lust for life and tried to get the most out of everyday special occasions.

"Let's make a delicious honey cake!"

"Clara, don't encourage gluttony!"

"Let's set up the Nativity, it's almost Christmas!"

"But it's the beginning of November. . . . Clara, don't be so flighty!"

"Let's go see who's walking by in the street!"

"Clara, I have never heard you say: 'Let's pray the rosary!'"

The rest of her family did not hold her in high esteem, either, because she baptized her cats with the names of her nieces and nephews.

"I've had it! Aunt Clara is always treating us just like the cats."

She celebrated her cats' weddings, baptisms, and birthdays with the same cake and candy that she prepared for her nieces and nephews. She didn't differentiate between them. The children's parents were always jealous that the aunt created this parallel between them. Aunt Clarita's unfulfilled maternal instinct had to spill over onto someone.

30

Aunt Clarita's cats were very refined Angoras, and she always lavished them with special treatment. As time went by, and especially because of the ongoing inbreeding among them, they began to degenerate and develop flaws until finally the mice started chasing the cats around. Aunt Clarita never allowed her cats to mate with others, influenced by the same attitude that her sister, Catalina, had toward her.

Juanito was born with three paws and a fourth barely formed, which made Aunt Clarita suffer a great deal, as she couldn't bear to watch Juanito walking on crutches. She ordered a balsa-wood leg from a cabinetmaker and fastened it to his back with two elastic bands. It took him many months to learn the complicated process of walking with the wooden leg.

"Come on, Juanito, learn to walk on your little wooden leg, be a good little boy. . . ."

Bruna the cat chose not to live in the house with the other cats; she lived on the roof, and her food had to be brought up to her every day on a very tall ladder; the Indian who cleaned Uncle Francisco's rooms risked his life going up and down it, cursing the animal's bad breeding the whole time.

"One of these days I'm going to kill that spoiled cat. . . ."

Lolita was born one-eyed. The socket of her nonexistent eye was always dripping pus, even though it was continually washed with rosemary water and other herbal solutions. Her whiskers kept moving in every direction, as if she were making faces, but she couldn't chase away the flies that were always buzzing around her, so Aunt Clarita had to make her an eye patch that she tied over one ear in the style of the princess of Eboli.

"Come on, Lolita, let me put on your eye patch!"

"She looks like a pirate!"

"Shush! Don't say that so loud! If she hears you, she won't want to wear anything."

When the nieces and nephews were little, the cats' bath was the most important event of the week. It was something that transcended the familiar walls around them and filled their spirits as if it were the twelfth night of Christmas. They were bathed on Thursdays so that the nieces and nephews could participate, along with one or two classmates who were invited along if they bribed the Catovils with enough gifts.

From the early morning hours, the patio became a fiesta, with three washbasins full of water warming in the sun. After the noon dinner they added hot water, some basins getting more than others, so that the water temperature in each would be exactly the same and the cats wouldn't feel a sudden change as they were passed from one to the other.

"Don't get the water dirty by putting your dirty hands in it!"

"We're just testing it to see if it's warm enough. . . ."

"Only I know when the temperature's right."

The first basin was filled with soapy water and flea powder, the second with pure water, and the third with fragrant eucalyptus leaves plus a dash of 4711 cologne.

All of the older nieces and nephews had the right to help with the bathing.

"Beat it, kids, you're too young to do this!"

The younger ones hardly dared to stick their fingertips quickly in the water and watched what the others were doing with envy, furious that they weren't old enough to handle the cats. As soon as the cats came in contact with the water, they went wild and tried to bite whatever was in front of them. At least they couldn't use their sharp claws, because their paws were covered with rabbit-fur gloves that Aunt Clarita had made to order in their size.

On first appearance it didn't seem possible for all seven cats to fit in the washbasin, but once they were in the water and their fur got wet, they looked much smaller. The cats metamorphosed into repulsive eels that twisted as if they were dancing a bizarre, diabolical dance, prodded by invisible whips.

"Meowwww, meowww, grrr!"

"What an uproar!"

"They're screeching like souls in hell!"

"Don't say that, that'll only make them madder!"

They passed from one washbasin to the other, always presenting the repulsive spectacle of slithering intestines being washed outside the stomach. As the cats were goaded by the thousand hands that enjoyed touching them, there was total confusion. Each person had been assigned his or her respective cat, but once in the water, they all felt the same. Their hands grabbed each other's hands, provoking riotous laughter. Aunt Clarita didn't take charge of any one cat; she helped everybody, going back and forth supervising the complicated operation, because often while the hands were grabbing each other under the water, one of the cats would take advantage of this careless moment to escape and the aunt had to be ready to catch it.

"He's escaping, Gabriel's escaping!"

"No, I'm not, I'm here with my cat!"

"Not you, Gabriel the cat!"

"I've got Gabriel the cat!"

"No, you've got Teresa!"

"That's not Teresa, that's Lola, see her eye patch!"

"Owww! Bruna bit me!"

"Which Bruna?"

"Juanito's leg has come loose!"

"Be careful! Don't pull his tail!"

The cats' dreadful howling filled every inch of the patio and climbed up to the roof as if they were calling all the cats in the world for help. The atmosphere filled with strange vapors and musky odors that excited people's spirits. The nieces and nephews forgot about the cats and pinched each other in a flurry of hands. It was all very noisy and confusing. Everyone ended up wet and laughing uncontrollably. The stupid fish in the fountain stretched its body to see everything better, and later on the "pisstatue" would die of sorrow watching the basins fall into disrepair because the cats had died, the children had grown, and Aunt Clarita slowly got older and forgot about the fun-filled Thursdays.

The whole patio was spattered with water, the imps withdrew from the rooftops, and everyone was happy.

"Boy, that was fun!"

"Even better than the other times!"

Once out of the water the cats were each placed on a towel and rubbed from top to bottom. Aunt Clarita climbed up to the eaves of the tile roof, grabbed three or four rays of sunlight, and directed them toward the patio so that the cats would dry quicker and not catch cold. Then their hair was combed and brushed. When they were dry and as fluffy as ever, they were given clean ribbons, yellow, green, or pink, tied around their necks with two bows. During Lent, at Aunt Catalina's insistence, they wore dark purple ribbons.

There were gray cats and black cats, running the gamut of shades of mourning. The animals were rather stupid, without the least bit of intelligence and with no other redeeming qualities besides their beautiful fur and their deep green eyes that sparkled like brightly lit windows with their treachery shining through.

"Aunt Clarita, Juan scratched me for no reason!"

"Which Juan, darling?"

"Which one do you think? The same one as always!"

In the bright daytime sun their pupils got small and round, and in darkness they grew like grains of wheat because the more light they could gather, the farther they could see.

They kept electric shocks hidden in their fur coats. They were mysterious thanks to their studied hypocrisy and their feline gait, skimming along the ground as if they were testing it first before walking on it. They let themselves be petted by the children, but they always found an opportune moment to claw the skin of an arm or a leg, leaving painful trails that conveyed fierceness and surprise.

"Owww, Lila scratched my leg!"

"Because you were bothering her, darling."

"No, Aunt, we were just playing, when suddenly . . ."

They would come over and rub up against a leg, looking for some affection, and when they got it and a hand was still buried in their fur, they'd slash out and run away howling as if the children had clawed them and not the other way round.

"What's going on with my cats?"

"They're scratching us for no reason at all."

"That can't be true. . . . For no reason at all!"

"I swear it's true, Aunt Clarita!"

"Why are you so mean to God's poor little animals who haven't done a thing to you, hmm?"

"That's not true, Aunt Clarita!"

"Why do you hit them, hmm?"

The cats were like those women who go out into the street looking for words that substitute for men's actions, the compliments that they are missing to round out their loneliness or their desire, the look that will wrap around their waist like a hug, and when they find it, they march away, putting their heart and soul into their hips and sending a cry of forced protest to the clouds. Those women who make wild displays of emotion about the honor that weighs so heavily on a certain part of their bodies and don't dare rid themselves of it because of the conventionalisms that are strangling them, while the poor masculine creatures are left with their mouths open, not knowing which side they should be on.

"Women!"

The cats were like them, like those flirtatious women, cowards, hungry, yet needing to take something like a wrong step, but without the consequences, or the comments, or the what-will-people-say-ism of the city folk.

Aunt Clarita had an old magazine with a photo of the city of Bubastis. Bubastis was the place where the ancient Egyptians preserved their cats, embalming them when they had stopped feeling the breezes of the Nile. She felt great admiration for the Egyptians because they had worshiped cats. The nieces and nephews called any place where a cat was buried a "bubasti." They knew a lot of things about all the felines in the world, from ferrets to mongooses. Thanks to Aunt Clarita they realized sooner than the adults that the sleeping city was not the only place on earth, that there were other places, and those other places were Bubastis, Paris, the Earthly Paradise, Egypt, the city of Ur of the Chaldeans, and the Mother Country, who was some kind of really big woman who put some earth down in the ocean and made it livable.

"Who is the Mother Country?"

"The one who gave us our language, our religion, and our customs."

"What's the Mother Country like?"

"Oh, big and magnificent!"

"Where is she?"

"On the other side of the ocean."

"And why did she go over there?"

After the cats forgot about having been bathed, Aunt Clarita brushed their teeth with tiny little brushes. The cats let her do this, and the kids took the opportunity to stick their noses in. The cats had small, sharp, white teeth, six incisors above and six below, in contrast with the canines, which were much larger and looked like daggers. On top, in the back, there were three sharp, triangular molars on each side, which fit into the corresponding depressions of those on the bottom, forming a much more efficient system than that of the meat grinder, which was always getting jammed and had to be cranked backward to be loosened.

Tired of working so hard on her cats, Aunt Clarita went to her room to lie down, and the children took advantage of this moment to grab the cats and wet their feet so they would leave their footprints on the floor as they walked down the long corridor. These footprints left a round wet spot surrounded by smaller round wet spots. It was a dangerous game because the cats ended up getting angry and distributing scratches to everyone. When the corridor was full of little wet spots, the kids had fun spitting on the floor and filling in the empty spaces with other little wets spots that they made with their fingertips. This was their Thursday-afternoon crossword puzzle. But they were already tired by then and didn't feel like laughing anymore; all their earlier emotions had run dry, and they waited, dreading the moment when Aunt Catalina would call them into her rooms to pray the rosary.

"The fun is over! Upstairs! Time to pray the rosary for the souls in purgatory!"

"Just a little longer!"

"Absolutely not, you've already had plenty of free time! Upstairs!"

The children bowed their heads and started to go upstairs, dragging their feet. Praying the rosary was the only sad, dark note on Thursdays.

31

Bruna always liked to test out everything that she was told, because in such an artificial world she didn't know what she could rely on. One day she wanted to know if it was really true that cats have nine lives. Aunt Clarita was not in the house; she had gone out to see what was new in the city's department stores. Bruna was bored; the young secretary she could spend some time with wasn't even there anymore. Aunt Catalina was busy saving her soul, and Mama Chana was in the garden, mending clothes.

One day Bruna grabbed Lola by the neck and, without giving it a second thought, threw her down onto the patio. They cat spun her tail in the air as if it were a rudder—it was understood that she would land correctly—spread out her paws, bounced a little on the stones, and ran away howling. . . . So cats really did have nine lives; the cat who lived on the roof jumped down and landed the same way.

But that day, one of them, perhaps caught unawares or because it had actually used up all nine of its lives, did not spin its tail in the air when Bruna threw her, and fell heavily to the patio as if she had thrown a blood-soaked shawl from the second floor. . . . The cat smashed into the flat rocks in the patio. The fish opened its eyes wide: this was murder. The water in the fountain froze: there was a limit to what the people in the house could get away with; the imps pulled their hats down over their eyes: this was too much. The cat was lying motionless on the rocks, facedown with its four legs spread out absurdly like a skin being laid out to dry. Its head was split open, and it wasn't gray, but black with blood.

Bruna ran like crazy to the garden and stopped in front of the well with the eye of the Devil, waiting to hear the voices that would be coming from it. Mama Chana stopped sewing and fixed her eye on her, saying:

"What have you done, little Bruna, what have you done, hmm?"

"Quiet, quiet!"

At that moment the false door in the big oak door opened and Aunt Clarita came in from the street. She saw the cat soaked with its own blood and understood that this was not a death from natural causes, because it was Tomasito, the smartest one. She wanted to back away when she saw how the cat's fangs, which had fallen out of its mouth, were growing in size and flying toward her threateningly. She wanted to defend herself, and she couldn't. The fangs ran through her clothing and pierced the middle of her chest, right below the cross of Caravaca that she always wore to protect herself against the Evil Eye, and it remained embedded in her flesh, still trying to push farther in.

Aunt Clarita cried over the loss of her cat. Uncle Francisco—who was still alive—didn't even know that he had been buried, even though they had told him about it many times.

"Francisco! Look what Bruna did!"

"What?"

"She killed Tomasito!"

"Yes, good . . . Tomasito . . ."

"But Francisco!"

"What?"

"It was murder!"

"Yes . . . murder . . ."

On the other hand, Aunt Catalina heard what happened and rushed right out of her private offices and surprised the nieces and nephews as they were trying to tiptoe back to their houses with their heads down. Furious, she made them turn back, and grabbing a fistful of the sand where the cats were supposed to attend to their needs but never did, she sprinkled it around the corridor. She made all the children kneel on the sand and pray the rosary for the souls in purgatory, because that was the longest of all the rosaries. . . .

"*Guambras pecata mundi,* you evil children! This is a crime! A crime! You have mortally sinned, and broken the Fifth Commandment! Who did it?"

All eyes turned toward Bruna.

"Child of the Devil! Murderer! You'll end up behind bars! You should be with the nuns of the Good Shepherd!"

On her knees before the implacable judge of her conscience and Aunt Catalina's penetrating stare, Bruna struggled to get comfortable on the tiny rocks that were boring into the thin skin of her kneecaps. She tasted the physical pain as if she were sucking on badly made lemon candy, bitter and sour at the same time, which she didn't dare spit out, curious to see for herself if she was capable of enduring it to the end. Desolate, she walked the paths of her conscience. She went back and forth between guilt and atonement. The death of the cat and the grains of sand that she was kneeling on had an unknown and slightly agreeable flavor: it was her first experience with masochism, because that's how guilt and pain are balanced. What hurt more than her knees was the pain that she had caused Aunt Clarita, without meaning to, because she loved her very much and had a special spiritual affinity with her. But she also thought how useless it was to try to settle such a debt with an act that did no one any good, because the humiliation and pain of kneeling fell into a void; and none of this made up for the satisfaction being derived from it by Aunt Catalina, who cared not about the cat or Aunt Clarita's pain, but only about her excessive urge for morality. What she felt inside herself was something imponderable that had nothing to do with the ridiculous punishment she was undergoing. Aunt Catalina spat out the *s*'s of the *ora pronobis,* and her sister was as silent as a stone statue, feeling the fangs hunting around for a comfortable place to stay and live inside of her forever.

Bruna was convinced that if the Devil, imps, and ghosts really did exist somewhere on earth, they must have been living in her aunts' and uncle's house. She was afraid that insanity was a contagious disease, as well as a congenital one that ran through her blood, and whose existence, like any living being's, would one day come to an end, at which point it would come out through the surface of her skin to take possession of people's actions and take over their minds, getting in through the obscure mechanism of hallucinations and wickedness. For the first time she was afraid of bearing the name "Catovil," and it pained her to visit the old family house.

The cat's burial was unforgettable; this was the first Angora to have died violently; the others would die of old age. Everyone remembered Bubastis and started talking about Egyptians and mummies. The cat was washed and perfumed. A cardboard box was found and emptied out. They made a small, beautiful little pillow to lay his broken head on. The box was carefully closed. They dug a very deep hole in the orchard. They tamped down the earth over the deceased and planted flowers to decorate the place, which was quite out of the way, nobody ever went there. Finally they took a cross, removed the Christ from it, put the Christ in the bottom of a drawer, and left the lonely, naked cross to cast its shadow across the cat's tomb.

"He met his end, as we all must do!"

"Have you really forgiven us, Aunt Clarita?"

"Yes, children, yes."

"Even Bruna?"

"Even Bruna."

After this incident the cats and the children settled the problem by erecting a wall of indifference between them. The children continued to participate in the bathing of the cats, but they kept their distance, which gradually increased until it became several yards and eventually went over to the next house. The cats stopped rubbing up against the children's legs. They were no longer interested in being petted, nor did they wait for the moment to scratch them; they just spied on them from afar. Their eyes shone more brightly, and some kind of hatred came from their whiskers.

After an appropriate amount of time, more or less the length of the period of mourning, Aunt Clarita officially pardoned the children. But a curtain of sadness fell between her and Bruna, her favorite niece, that was never lifted. From that point on they stopped looking deeply into one another's eyes, and when they held hands, nothing was passed from one to the other. The cat with its split head lay between them and made it very difficult for them to communicate.

Aunt Clarita began to get old: she forgot to curl her hair at night, she went for a long time without going into the street, she stopped dyeing her hair, she forgot about the face mask for the wrinkles. When her subscription to *Au Bon Marché* ran out, she didn't renew it; she stopped watering the geraniums and feeding the canaries, and when she got a run in her last pair of silk stockings, she tried on some cotton stockings and found that they lasted longer and kept her warmer, and she started using them. She withstood her loneliness with a sadness that seemed like resignation and ended up seeking the company of the only person who lived in the house with her, which was Mama Chana, who watched her from the depths of her dark thoughts and the plans that she had hatched years before.

Bruna also began to feel alone, because she had grown up and the old family house seemed much smaller. Aunt Clarita's circle was closed, with her tiny body and her memories. Bruna's circle had scaled the roof and was aiming beyond the mountains.

32

Aunt Clarita outlived her brother and sisters, many of her nieces and nephews, the cats and the geraniums that she once cared for. She stayed alone in the big old house, and when the years started to weigh on her shoulders, and especially on her kidneys, she had to get up at night more often than usual and go down the corridor toward the bathroom, pushing aside the gloom with her hands and stumbling over the ghosts who were playing cutthroat games of hopscotch and jacks on the floor.

"Let me through! Let me through!"

"Go ahead. . . ."

"But you're everywhere."

She decided that she had the right to some small comfort and made the mountain come to Mohammed, having the bathroom come to her instead of her going to the bathroom. She had a bathtub put in her bedroom, which was the only livable room in the house. She got rid of the bed, which was useless anyway because of her insomnia, and put it in a corner with the mermaid and the 245 swords of the defenders of the faith. She put the bathtub underneath the window, where the rays of sunlight fell from beyond the mountains. She covered it with a cheerful fabric sewn with gracefully curving festoons and pictures of little houses with orange roofs, smoking chimneys, and trees on both sides. She upholstered the inside of the bathtub with the same fabric.

She had an oval-shaped mattress and sheets and blankets that were shaken out and folded up every morning as if this were an ordinary, everyday bed.

"Aunt Clarita! Is this a bed or a tub, hmm?"

"This is my bed."

"And you're going to sleep here?"

"Yes, my boy, yes."

"Well, you're never going to fall out of it. . . ."

When she had to get up at night, she took care of her body's legitimate needs by lifting up the mattress and taking the plug out of the drain. After some maneuvers that sometimes made her lose her balance, she would get into the correct position and do what she wanted to do. . . . Then she'd turn on the water faucet and the stream would wash right down the drain and leave her in peace. Afterward she'd sprinkle a little 4711 cologne around the room and on the damp parts of the bed, find the best position in the bathtub bed, and sink into the world of simple, easy things: she went to Paris in the small coach and drank champagne in a café on the Champs-Elysées, accompanied by some of her old suitors.

"What a bright, sunny afternoon! What a soft, gentle breeze!"

"Your hands are softer, my dear Clarita. . . ."

She bathed the cats in the warm afternoon sun and sprinkled them with perfume.

"Pass me the cologne!"

"Mmmmm, Tomasito smells so good!"

She listened to the poems that her brother, Francisco, had written for her.

"Sit down, Clarita, I'm going to read what I have written for you. Make yourself comfortable in the armchair."

"Thank you, Francisco, you're the best brother in the world. . . ."

She saw her sister, Catalina, fitting her in the lacy folds of her bridal gown and the nieces and nephews dressed up as flower girls and page boys, ready to participate in her wedding ceremony.

"Clarita, you're beautiful!"

"Aunt Clarita, you look like a queen!"

"Don't forget to walk slowly when you enter the church."

She sat in the rocking chair in the courtyard, reading a fashion magazine, surrounded by cats, canaries, and geraniums, while the children played without fighting and sang the nursery rhyme with *matan-tirun tirun-lá* in it. Then the bathtub coach entered the tunnel of loneliness and took hours to get through it, while the nearby church bells rang out the hours and the half hours all night long and into the early morning, until the sun came out; and then she realized that she hadn't slept at all that night and that all the following nights would be the same.

"I can't sleep, I can't!"

"Tonight I'll make you some tea with lettuce leaves."

"Thank you, Mama Chana."

And so, between her fussing and worrying—not about her conscience, which was as smooth as a mirror, but about neatness, because she resembled a cat in that regard—she ended up staying alone and marking the calendar with a red cross on the days that the kids had been charitable enough to visit her for ten minutes.

"The kids haven't come."

"They're thankless and ungrateful!"

"Maybe they're sick. . . . Mama Chana, go next door and ask about them."

"They're not sick or anything, what's happening is—what's happening."

The nieces and nephews grew up faster as she got older until the day came that nobody remembered that it was Thursday anymore. They started going bravely near the well and laughing at having been so naive. Then they started to notice that the tales and stories that Aunt Clarita told, pouring her soul into them, were deadly dull. They realized that the big old house was sad and mildewy. Then they said that it was crazy for a poor old woman to sleep in a bathtub, and they left her alone with her painful stockpile of memories and with a strong craving for death when she felt the cat's fangs in her chest that had grown and taken over her insides.

Later on, Aunt Clarita saw other nieces and nephews appear in the house; they were Mama Chana's children. . . . When they had fun they filled the house with metallic laughter like the crashing of rusty old cans.

"Chana! What are they doing here?"

"They've come to visit. . . ."

"I don't want any noise, tell them to leave!"

"Well, you see, the poor little ones . . ."

Mama Chana had five children who were not born the way all other mortals are: they came into the world dressed as choirboys. Their father was the parish sacristan, the one who supplied Mama Chana with rose petals for Aunt Catalina's salads. It was possible that one of them might have been Uncle Francisco's child: one morning, without knowing how or when, he woke up in Mama Chana's room, without thinking of it, wanting it, or understanding it.

"What is this? Where am I? What am I doing here? Help! I've been kidnapped! They've stolen my matchboxes!"

"Quiet down, for God's sake, quiet down, Don Francisco!"

"Ah . . . you're that Chana woman!"

"Yes, and you are in my bed!"

"Whaaaat!"

Maybe Mama Chana tied him up with Saint Ambrose's shoelaces, and the strings squeezed him so tightly that he shrank in size, so she could put him inside a matchbox and keep him deep in the pocket of her old apron until the bells chimed midnight: the hour of spells and witchcraft.

Everyone knew that Mama Chana was part witch and part folk healer. She had made a pact with the Devil—not at the cost of her soul, but at the cost of a few sacks of corn. With the income from this pact she bought a few rows of land and planted corn; when the harvest came, she sold the corn and paid off the debt.

Mama Chana lived for more than a hundred years, putting herself into the family stories and tangling them up as she saw fit. In spite of her lies, Bruna loved her because she opened the doors to the past and because the stories that fell from her lips held back the passage of time and gave life to the dead.

When Mama Chana got tired of life, she showed her children and her grandchildren the document signed by Uncle Francisco in the bitter moment of death, the document whereby he recognized Mama Chana's children as his own. The document was so confusing and written so diabolically that the letters jumped off the page and re-formed however they pleased, so that each person who read the document interpreted it however they wanted to. Moreover, it was written with strange words and unknown symbols. The Catovils were no good at fighting, and they let María Illacatu's greatly diminished fortune go to Mama Chana's grandchildren.

"That document is illegal, completely illegal!"

"But here's his signature!"

"That signature is different from all his other signatures!"

"That's because it's the signature of a dying man!"

"Dying men don't sign their names!"

"He signed it, and in front of witnesses!"

"Where are the witnesses?"

"In their tombs, that's where!"

Aunt Clarita spent the last years of her life among people she didn't know who insisted on calling her "Aunt."

"And don't call me 'Aunt,' I'm not related to you!"

It was evident that these weren't Catovils; they didn't have the reckless blood of her nieces and nephews, never mind of her ancestors. They were out of place in the house and in the sleeping city. They must have been descendants of King Midas. Whenever they bought a lottery ticket they won the grand prize, which meant that some regulations had to be established regarding lottery ticket sales.

"Lottery tickets! Lottery tickets!"

"The Chanos can't buy any?"

"No, they can't buy any, the junta has forbidden it. . . ."

"Then give me a *huachito*."

212

One time, one of them was poking the earth with a stick while he was doing what María the Twenty-third's Indians did—because Aunt Clarita had forbidden the intruders from using what was left of the bathroom—and found a piece of leather in the ground. He kept digging with another stick, because the first one had broken, and found the cover of a black leather chest. He opened the chest with another stick and saw that it was filled to the rim with pure gold coins. . . . It was the same chest that had cost Uncle Panchito his life, with the months and months of preparations and the disappointment of finding it only to watch it get up and run away before the shocked eyes of the men who dug up the treasure. . . .

And so Mama Chana's descendants, whom everyone called the Chanos, kept accumulating more and more treasure. They married rich women who made them widowers the day after the wedding, leaving them willing and able to marry more rich women. They bought useless things that turned out to be treasures. If they held out their hands to see if it was raining, a few drops of gold would land in their upturned palms. They lent money, shamelessly charging interest, with the approval and respect of the people in the sleeping city, who stood by them more out of convenience than conviction. The Chanos were feared, but not loved. They displayed their wealth brazenly, trampling on shabby clothes, jeering at hunger, and turning up their noses at misery.

They had a dimly lit hardware store that was as dark as the cave of Ali Baba's forty thieves. They stocked nails, pills for *soroche,* tacks, old shoes, tools, lard and candle grease, screws, dyes. People said enviously:

"The Chanos sure have a nose for business."

"Of course they do! That's all they live for! Have you ever seen a Jesus Christ, an Aristotle, a Christopher Columbus, or a Beethoven running a hardware store?" came the pained response from one of the Catovils who was vainly trying to survive by sidestepping poverty.

213

The Chanos' wealth was offensive, excessive, over the top. They fought against sobriety and good taste; they were the type that would put three lamps in a row next to the couch, several vases on the same table, enormous gilded plaques on their front doors that announced from a distance:

"We live here, not somebody else."

They would wear a gold watch on a chain and a platinum wristwatch, too. The Chanos wore as many diamonds and rubies as a jewelry store display window just to work in the hardware store.

"Ooh, look how the Chanos sparkle!"

"Out of the way if God hasn't given you any crops this year!"

"I'm two centavos short. . . ."

"Then I'm not selling it!"

"It's only two centavos!"

"You'd think it was two thousand. . . ."

"Newly rich sons of b—"

"Step aside if you can't afford it!"

"I'm sick, I need the pills. . . . I don't have the money. . . . Can I pay you tomorrow?"

"So buy them tomorrow."

"Such fine people! Living in such abundance! They're so fabulous!"

"Such poor people. . . . Living on borrowed time. . . . They're so humble. . . ."

33

Bruna passed the time having fun, getting bored, and doing a little of everything with the girls her age who were dazzled by the light of their convictions, who never dared to question them out of fear that a lightning bolt would come down from heaven and punish them for the audacity of daring to think for themselves. They kept right on believing that eating avocado with sugar was a mortal sin, but they couldn't possibly explain why.

"Let's just eat a little bit, to see what happens!"

"I bet nothing will happen, but we'll be committing a mortal sin."

"But something has to happen for it to be a sin. . . . You have to feel something . . . something has to happen. . . ."

"Let's eat a bit!"

"Eating a bit is no joke. You're like Eve in the Garden of Eden."

"And look what happened. . . ."

They organized lots of dances and trips to the countryside, where they sang songs whose words had offensive meanings, which they repeated without anyone saying anything because they had been sung for years and nobody had said anything back then. The all-girl dances were simply horrible.

"Let's have a party and invite some boys!"

"No, no boys! What would my parents say!"

"You don't have to tell them that we invited boys. . . ."

Sometimes Bruna danced with a girlfriend, and between turns

she felt a growing uneasiness when someone rubbed against her body, but since people told her so much about other things and nothing about that, she tried to overcome it.

"See how they're having such good, clean fun!"

"There's no danger as long as they do it like this."

It was seen as the most natural thing in the world, the way the girls stroked each other's hair and held hands, sending out sweat and sensations.

Without knowing how or when, a gust of what was happening on the other side of the mountains blew into the sleeping city. The adults were extremely worried because they saw that the principles they had used to educate their children were in danger and felt that the stability of their households was shifting; they couldn't understand how the new generation could fish for compliments while they were dancing to such shrill and disjointed music.

"This isn't music, it's jungle noise!"

"The young people are going astray!"

In the city it started to look bad if one wasn't in fashion. The younger generation was caught in a genuine mental chaos between their actions and their desires. Modernity was a give-and-take that was full of contradictions, without any base on which to build what they wanted. They were innocent victims of *soroche,* but they were truly afraid of seeming old-fashioned. The term "old-fashioned" became a synonym for immoral even for the old folks, who heard it so much that they began to feel uncomfortable and realized that the sleeping city was the last holdout in a world that, like it or not, was round.

You didn't travel by mule anymore; now it was by train and even by flying over the roads and houses. Thanks to this, communications were faster, and bundles of magazines arrived regularly and were devoured by eyes that were eager to see more things. In the living rooms of people who had the means, a table was set aside for a radio, and the whole family would gather around to listen and talk about how the voice came right through the walls.

All this happened so suddenly that nobody took charge of instructing people how to live through it. The young people built their baseless, chaotic world; the old people crossed themselves and shut themselves in their shells, and the few people who had minds like Bruna began to develop a delicious skepticism.

People went to the movies. They heard about some feminist endeavors and the latest in sports. The old and stupid saying "A sound mind in a sound body" became highly fashionable. Women started going to swimming pools to free themselves of some fatty tissue, although they didn't yet dare to use the indecent bathing suits that they saw in the magazines. In Bruna's high school they set up a swimming pool to help give them sound minds, but the girls had to swim around in horrible long blue shirts that reached to their ankles. When they got into the water to swim, many of them managed to float, but on contact with the water, the enormous shirts sometimes acted like air bubbles and rose up to their throats, leaving their bodies as naked as the pistils of a gigantic flower, which was why they were permanently forbidden from diving. . . .

When the Polish ballerina left holding her brother's hand, never to return to the city, as a way of saying good-bye, and of holding back the tears that were about to flow from both of their eyes, she said to Bruna:

"I've left a gift for you and your friends."

"Don't go!"

"We'll die if we stay here. . . ."

To ease her pain and to keep from crying like a little girl whose toy has been taken away, Bruna opened the package, and the surprise made her smile: bathing suits! She divided them up among the girls.

"Here."

"What is it?"

"A gift from Milka."

"For me?"

"Yes."

"How odd that Milka gave me a gift and she doesn't even know me!"

When it was her day to go swimming, Bruna stayed at home because she didn't feel like doing anything. Her brother's extremely short visit with his wife had left her crushed and confused. Were the people from other places so different that they didn't even rest after such a long trip before running off to somewhere else?

The rest of the girls managed to sneak into the pool, because otherwise they couldn't use Milka's gifts. They jumped into the water with a combination of prudish laughter and the satisfaction of having the audacity to be the pioneers of a fashion that would one day be generally accepted.

Once they were in the pool, the clothes disappeared as if by magic. . . . Bruna, without knowing it, had played a trick on them. The bathing suits were made of soluble material and vanished on contact with water. . . . The Polish ballerina sure knew how to choose gifts for the girls in the sleeping city.

And the city would keep on sleeping until they invented gigantic fans that could push the air that carried the mysterious ravages of *soroche* off toward the jungle. The *soroche* got into the pool and covered the girls' bodies, and the girls stayed in the pool for nearly two days, praying hopefully for an angel to come down from heaven with towels to cover their frigid, naked bodies.

"Who's going to get out first and get us some towels?"

"Not me!"

"Me neither!"

"Never!"

"We're going to die!"

"God, send us a miracle!"

Their prayers were not answered. They stayed in the cold water for days, turning purple from cold. Unable to confront the total nudity of their bodies, they stayed there, hugging each other for heat, like a gigantic octopus that was dying of panic and cold. They didn't even dare come out in the darkness of night from the fear of seeing each other naked and the horror of feeling certain parts of their bodies being looked at.

The swimming pool was in an out-of-the-way place where nobody could hear their cries for help. On the other hand, their cries weren't very convincing, because—in case someone actually showed up—they couldn't find the words to explain why they were naked. Who would believe that they had gotten into the water wearing bathing suits and now they weren't? Sometimes they felt guilty themselves for having done something at odds with the morality that had been drilled into them. Overwhelmed with fear and terror, they waited for death to come; and if it came, what would the people say when they found them in this condition?

"What do we do?"

"We wait for death."

"Like this, naked?"

"Let's get out of here!"

"I'm not going first!"

"Me neither!"

"Never!"

The police finally intervened. Everyone was looking for them, and nobody could find them. Somebody walked by and finally saw them. Even so, they refused to get out until they were given clothes. Nearly frozen, they got dressed in the water . . . and came out dripping into the arms of their saviors.

When Bruna heard what had happened, she bit her lip until she bled. The distance between herself and her friends was already too great.

"You gave them that diabolical clothing!"

"I didn't know. . . ."

"Only you could do such a thing!"

This matter was harshly criticized. Once again a lurid story was written across the facade of the Catovils' house, as it was in the days when they said so many things about Camelia the Tearful. The girls were compared with María Goretti and declared from the church pulpits to be martyrs for purity.

"These heroic girls preferred death to committing the sin of impurity. . . ."

And Bruna's best friend—the one who put little pebbles in her shoes as part of her penance, who was never in a foul mood but always had a smile on her lips as if she were a dewy flower, who looked at life with her eyes wide open with surprise, always asking why without understanding the answers, who wandered around lost amid so much confusion and for that reason never spoke, because she was like a frightened bird, and who was Bruna's favorite of them all because she occupied a tiny sphere of life full of unknowns—that one, that exact one, died of pneumonia.

Bruna lost her whole life's work in a few hours. The sleeping city suddenly woke up just to accuse her. The twisted streets, entwined like tangled woolen threads, were boiling with gossip. The golden churches with their tall towers called the people into Mass, ringing out her name with the adjective "murderer." The people, shaken out of their *soroche,* pointed their fingers at her. The imps, ghosts, and witches who had been relegated to oblivion came back to rule the minds of the people in the city.

"But it's not possible, she's only fifteen years old!"

"Nevertheless, she's still a murderer."

"The Catovils have always been ready to cause a scandal!"

"It's in their blood!"

Bruna decided to lose herself, to eliminate herself from the face of the earth, and without thinking twice, she started walking, and walking, following the same route that her great-grandfather the bishop of Villa-Cató had taken. She knew that if she walked a little faster, she would meet Gabriel and Milka at some turn in the road, join them, and continue traveling around the world with them.

When her strength failed, she stopped for air. She turned to look back at the sleeping city, and she couldn't find it. She climbed to the top of a hill and looked for it everywhere, but the city wasn't there. She looked for the church towers with their pointy belfries, and they weren't there, either. She retraced her steps. She reached the place where she knew the city had been, with its streets, its houses, its inhabitants, its hatreds, its hypocrisies, its sins, and couldn't find a thing. . . .

A gust of wind that had an unfamiliar smell, as if *soroche* had never existed, brought a piece of paper with it. Bruna rushed to grab it because it was the only sign that could point her toward what she was looking for. The paper was a piece of a page from the Bible that seemed to have been torn away at random and that read:

I WANT TO GO AND SEE IF YOUR DEEDS ARE EQUAL TO THE RUMOR THAT HAS REACHED MY EARS. . . .

She seemed to understand that it was a verse having to do with the destruction of Sodom and Gomorrah and bent her head, overwhelmed with pity; she understood the reason for the city's punishment and lost herself walking in the direction of sunrise.

Epilogue

Bruna left her adolescence behind as if it were an old piece of ragged clothing, as if her fully grown and developed body were trying to tear through the fabric. She freed herself from her memories because she needed to find some balance in her life while she fought ardently and tenaciously, emerging bruised and hurt but finally whole and happy with herself, conscious of the fact that life was the greatest gift that one could have, and it was worth getting bruised for it. If you only lived once, it was necessary to feel fully like a human, a person, a woman.

She achieved this when she left the city and never saw the fog of *soroche* again. She saw that there were other worlds beyond that hill of beans. She heard rumors about other latitudes where people suffered, enjoyed, were silent with fright or with terror, and evolved with dizzying speed.

The marble towers where she had been walled in, during the process of being turned into a mummy or a victim of *soroche*, came tumbling down one after the other. Sometimes a moment of deep thought, or a sleepless night, was enough to explore the foundations of a belief, find that they were made of sand, and see how the building that had seemed impregnable crumbled. The ironclad principles that she had been taught were nothing more than the whims a decrepit generation had imposed in order to maintain the size and strength of its personal sphere of power, a generation unwilling to see its errors, not brave enough to admit them, much less correct them.

"Parental authority is endangered. . . ."

"A father's authority isn't imposed, it rules."

"You have to dominate youthful rebelliousness. . . ."

"If youth weren't rebellious, we'd all end up hunchbacked from staring at the ground so much. . . ."

"The children want to order *us* around. . . ."

"The children want a fresh, clean place of their own where they can live."

While looking for a place in the world to live, she grew in stature and with the weight of life and found more reasons for being who she was. While sifting through her beliefs and tossing them away, she found that they were rooted in her emotions and nothing else. The ghosts, beliefs, miracles, and prejudices were all left behind with Aunt Clarita's cats. She believed in what she loved. She couldn't be judged for not having supernatural eyesight. She believed in a God who was not made in her image, or in the image of any human being, from any age or from any place. He was what He was. . . .

She knew that the world is big, that human beings have more stature than they seem to have, and that man and only man is the measure of all things. . . . Even Aunt Catalina, the poor thing . . . would have looked at things differently and cataloged her circumstances differently.

"Nobody was guilty of anything, it was *el soroche!*"

"Nobody taught anyone how to live, because nobody wanted to learn."

She cast her fears aside and dedicated herself to loving what the people of the city had disfigured and to exalting what they had slandered.

"A young, healthy body is prettier naked than dressed."

"Sex with love is the most perfect means of communication."

But she saw that the world was a seething mass of ambitions, and she left it all behind: working and working to get rich so that you could leave an inheritance that no one would thank you for, because the value of "having" would disappear one day. . . . In the face of the eternal misery of her fellow creatures, who never wanted to understand anything, who distorted the most beautiful acts and then interpreted even the most subtle acts in their own way, a curtain of compassion had to be drawn: those poor people. . . .

She saw that the struggle between the generations was a pointless spectacle as long as neither one defined the limits of their own spheres of life. It was like asking an elm tree to produce pears! How could one generation, educated with and for their myths, be able to confront another generation that came out of the maternal womb with values that they would never feel or understand?

Hippies, psychedelics, and rebels without a cause wouldn't appear for a very long time on the face of the earth. . . .

Translator's Notes

Prologue

8 *higuera negra* Castor-oil plant.

Chapter 2

14 *García Moreno* President of Ecuador (1861–65 and 1869–75). A dictatorial leader and religious conservative, he is generally credited with helping to modernize the country.

17 *Eugenio Espejo* Eugenio de Santa Cruz y Espejo (1747–95) was in fact of native Ecuadorian ("Indian") descent; he graduated in medicine and civil law and became the foremost essayist of the period, writing in favor of Ecuadorian independence from Spain. This landed him in prison, where he died.

24 *ñusta* Quichua word meaning "princess."

24 *chasqui* Quichua word for a runner who transported messages for the Incas.

Chapter 3

34 *caca de gallina* The children's nickname for their aunt; rhymes with "Catalina" and means "chicken shit."

Chapter 6

50 *mono . . . mona* Male and female monkeys.

51 *payachucho* Quichua word for a large, black butterfly; literally means "death's corner."

Chapter 8

60 *Bello-Animal* The name of this brothel vulgarizes somewhat the phrase *el bello sexo* ("the fair sex") into "the fair animal."

Chapter 9

72 *Rocinante* Don Quixote's horse; the name means "broken-down nag."

Chapter 10

76 *toronjil . . . serenita* Toronjil ("balm-gentle") is an herb, and *serenita* (diminuitive of "serene") is a tea made from a mixture of herbs; both are supposed to soothe the nerves.

Chapter 11

79 *llamingo* From the Quichua word *llamingu,* a relative of the llama.

Chapter 12

84 *Alvarito* The diminutive form of Alvaro, meaning "little Alvaro."

Chapter 15

104 *Carreño's* Manuel Antonio Carreño (1812–74), Venezuelan writer and politician whose *Manual de urbanidad* (*Guide to Manners*) was widely adopted as a schoolbook throughout Latin America.

Chapter 18

114 *centavos* A centavo is one one-hundredth of a sucre, the primary unit of Ecuadorian currency.

Chapter 21

139 *guarichas* Quichua word for women who traveled around with the armies in order to serve the soldiers' many needs.

Chapter 22

142 *Guambras peccata mundi* A mixture of Quichua and Latin meaning, roughly, "sinful boys."

147 *sucres* The sucre is the primary unit of Ecuadorian currency.

Chapter 23

151 tapeworm The original uses *cuica*, Quichua for tapeworm.

Chapter 27

174 *Girolamo Savonarola* "Terrifyingly severe" Italian Dominican monk (1452–98) who burned manuscripts, paintings, and other works of art that he deemed offensive, and who was eventually hanged for antipapal schism and heresy.

Chapter 28

187 *tea of mercy* A tea brewed with poisonous herbs used as a form of euthanasia.

Chapter 29

191 *cholo* A person of mixed European and native Ecuadorian ancestry;

this term describes at least 40 percent of the population, but Catalina's usage of it is clearly derogatory.

195 *she baptized her cats with the names of her nieces and nephews* In Ecuadorian culture, naming a pet after someone is an insult to that person.

Chapter 30

197 *princess of Eboli* Ana de Mendoza, princesa de Eboli (1540–92), one of the richest women in Spain during the reign of Philip II. She was famous for the black eye patch she wore over her right eye socket.

Chapter 31

204 *cross of Caravaca* An old Quiteño name for a cross with two horizontal bars.

Chapter 32

212 *huachito* Quichua word for a single piece of a lottery ticket. In Ecuador, a lottery ticket is actually a whole sheet of tickets with the same lottery number. One can buy one or more *huachitos,* but it takes a lot of money to buy the whole sheet.

Chapter 33

220 *María Goretti* An Italian saint canonized in 1950 who died for the sake of her purity.